TABBY OR NOT TABBY

A WHISKERS AND WORDS MYSTERY
BOOK TWO

ERYN SCOTT

KRISTOPHERSON
PRESS
Publishing

For a town that's as cute as a button, there sure is a lot of murder.

Louisa Henry's dream bookshop is up and running. On a trip to deliver a book to one of her customers, Lou stumbles upon the man's dead body. The police are sure it's a suicide, but Lou has questions. Clues at the scene and details about the man's life just don't seem to add up.

The fact that the dead man was the town bully is only one of many things that gives Lou pause. Are the police jumping to the conclusion of suicide so they don't have to arrest the person who did everyone a favor?

Lou's also busy helping her best friend, Willow, with preparations for the high school's annual Spring Fling. But during her time at the drafty old building, Lou finds secrets hidden away no one was meant to see, and she learns her new town might be hiding more than she first thought.

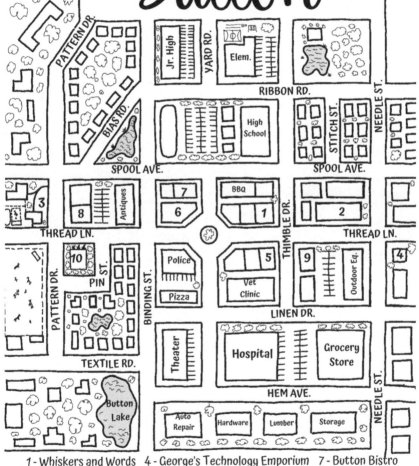

Welcome to Button

1 - Whiskers and Words   4 - George's Technology Emporium   7 - Button Bistro
2 - Material Girls   5 - Bean and Button Coffeehouse   8 - Pet Store   9 - Bakery
3 - Willow and Easton's houses   6 - The Upholstered Button   10 - Old Mansion

CHAPTER 1

L ouisa Henry should've been smiling. It was a gorgeous spring Sunday in the small town of Button—the kind of day that makes a person stop, tilt their head back, and let the sun warm their face.

Brilliant morning sun streamed through the front windows of a bookshop called Whiskers and Words, bathing a sleeping white cat in warm rays. The cat was deaf, so he didn't hear the chatter of customers. He curled a paw to cover his face as he readjusted his position, one leg dangling off the short stack of books acting as his bed.

It's not unusual to see a cat inside a shop, especially a shop that sells books. What was unusual about this business was the fact that the white cat in the window was just one of the many felines inside.

Sure, the shop held all the normal bookstore fare. Customers still milled through the aisles, getting lost in the beautiful covers, poring over summaries of the stories held within the pages. Other patrons had already been sucked into new worlds, lost to their surroundings as they sat and read.

The difference in Whiskers and Words was that the bearded

man, sitting with a paperback held open in one hand, used his other to stroke a purring gray tabby cat. A young girl kneeling to get a better look at the newest book in a series she loved laughed as a black cat rubbed up against her leg, almost pushing her over. And a woman perusing titles in the new-release section of the shop scrunched her fingers into the soft fur of a lovable orange tabby, planting a kiss on his head as she stopped to read the back cover of a best-selling science fiction novel.

An old man who came every day at the same time settled into a love seat, flicking open a newspaper. As if on cue, a white-and-orange cat jumped into his lap. She was the type of cat who hid from most others, but something about the old man in the bowler hat with the fluffy gray eyebrows brought her out of her shell.

Whiskers and Words was a bookshop, sure, but it was also a rescue-cat sanctuary. It was a cozy place for previously unwanted cats to wait until they found a new home. Adoption profiles for each cat hung inside the shop, telling potential adopters each cat's name as well as their likes and dislikes. They had literary names like Anne Mice, Purrt Vonnegut, and Catnip Everdeen.

The only cat without an adoption profile was the deaf white cat, Sapphire. He belonged to Lou.

Louisa was the owner of said shop. The peaceful sight before her should've made her break into a huge grin. After all, it had been her dream to own her own bookstore. Helping cats without homes find love and stability at the same time as selling books had only made that dream sweeter.

But as she hung up the shop phone, Lou frowned.

Part of the scowl she wore was thanks to the title she held in her hand. It was a book called *Why You Shouldn't Care About Other People*. She'd flipped through the pages, and it not only contained selfish, close-minded advice, but it also held a section at the back for readers to journal. The journal pages were even more disturbing. They included a place to list all the people the reader hated and the reasons.

"What are you so sour about?" The old man in the bowler hat glanced up from his newspaper. "I can feel your negativity hit me from across the room," he said, pointing at Lou accusingly.

Lou relaxed her face, unaware of how tight it had become. "Sorry, Silas." She blinked. "I just can't seem to get ahold of the customer who ordered this book, and I'd really like to get it out of my shop, if I'm being honest," she explained, revealing the second reason she'd been scowling.

"Who ordered it?" Silas asked, his fluffy gray eyebrows furrowing along with his already wrinkled forehead.

"Someone named Credence Crowley," Lou said, reading the name off the order slip. "He ordered over the phone, but the billing address he gave is local."

After living in Button for almost two months at that point, Lou was learning the names of all the streets and recognized Needle Street right away.

"Credence?" Silas spat out the name, causing Catnip Everdeen to vault from his lap at the outburst. The old man grumbled an apology to the cat but turned his attention back to Lou. "Why would he order a book? He can't read."

The woman who'd been wandering the aisles with the orange cat in her arms stopped and snorted. "Of course Credence can read, Silas." She rolled her eyes. But if Lou had been waiting for Hannah to jump to this Credence man's defense, she was mistaken. "How else would he be able to write those terrible opinion pieces he submits to the paper every month?"

Silas let out a deep chuckle. "Right. Good point."

A disheveled man who was younger than Lou entered the shop, darting back to the kids' section without making eye contact with anyone. The conversation paused as the group of customers watched him. Hannah's daughter, Sage, stopped petting The Great Catsby as she and the black cat watched the man enter the children's section.

"Honestly, Lou, it sounds like a good thing Credence won't

answer," the bearded man named Forrest said. His voice was as deep and velvety as the coat of the gray cat curled in his lap. "You don't want to do business with that man if you can help it."

"Who is he?" Lou asked.

"He owns Crowley Auto Repair down on Hem Avenue," the man said.

"Listen to Forrest," Hannah said. "Credence is nothing but trouble."

The man who'd darted inside moments ago walked up to the checkout counter, gripping a copy of *Goodnight Moon*. His eyes were rimmed with dark circles and his brown hair was mussed. He held the book forward. "We can't find our copy anywhere, and the triplets won't sleep unless they hear this at least seven times," he said, his voice froggy.

Lou took the picture book and rang it up, her heart going out to the obviously tired father.

"What are we talking about? Who's trouble?" the man asked as he readied his wallet.

"Credence." Silas barked out the name.

The tired father flinched.

Forrest shook his head. "Silas, you know better than to talk about that man around Timothy." Forrest was a local psychologist. His deep baritone voice and tranquil manner seemed to calm everyone he met.

Everyone except Timothy, Lou noticed. The tired father's posture was just as pinched as before he'd heard the name, if not more. Lou told him the amount for the book, and he handed over a card.

"We're sorry, Timothy." Hannah tilted her head to the side in pity. "We shouldn't have brought up *that man* around you." Hannah emphasized her avoidance of Credence's name, almost as if he were Lord Voldemort.

"It's okay," Timothy said, looking decidedly *not* okay. He grabbed his card from the reader once the transaction finished and took the book without a bag, leaving before Lou could even thank him for his purchase.

"What was that all about?" Lou asked, eyes wide.

Hannah wrinkled her nose. "Timothy had a bad run-in with Credence a couple of weeks ago. I don't think he's over it yet."

"His wallet definitely isn't." Silas let out a low chuckle.

"Even if this Credence guy is bad," Lou said with a glance down at the book he'd ordered—the title only supported what the other locals were telling her about his character—"I still need to deliver the book he ordered." She thought back to their phone conversation.

The title he'd ordered had alarmed her, but he'd mentioned that he was ordering from her shop because he liked what she was doing for the cats. He was a cat lover himself and chatted about his own beloved cat for a while before ending the call.

"Make sure that sleazeball pays you," Silas said, wagging a stubby finger. "Don't let him say he's going out to the car to grab his wallet or nothin'. He'll try to give you the slip."

"He already paid for it," Lou said. "That's the one reason I'm trying so hard to get in touch with him." *And I really don't want this terrible book sitting in my shop any longer than it needs to*, she added to herself. "Maybe he's just busy at work. I can run it by the auto repair shop." She ran out that way a few times each week.

"Don't bother. It'll be closed until tomorrow, at least," Hannah said. "It was his birthday yesterday. I heard him announce it at the grocery store on Thursday when he was buying a cake."

Lou pursed her lips, unsure why that meant his shop would be closed.

"Credence always takes at least three days off around his birthday," Forrest explained, seeing Lou's confusion.

"Oh, good for him?" Lou phrased it as a question, since saying anything nice about the man seemed to be frowned upon with the locals.

Silas scratched at his nose.

"Not really," Forrest said, wincing like it was difficult for him to say something mean. "I'm guessing he bought a fifth of vodka along with that cake." Forrest checked with Hannah, who nodded in confirmation.

"He spends his birthday weekend getting wasted in his house," Silas chimed in, saying the hard truth Forrest was having trouble voicing. "A day to get drunk, a day to hair the dog, and a day to recover."

"Oh, well." Lou checked the calendar behind the register. "It's Sunday, so he should be back to normal tomorrow. I can try calling again then, right?"

Hannah widened her eyes and walked away, Silas tsked, and Forrest looked down at his book.

That seems like a no, Lou thought with a sigh. She stashed the book on the shelf under the computer once more.

"Okay," Hannah said, "it's time for us to go." She set down the orange cat named Purrt Vonnegut. "Sage, let's head out," she called to the little girl who'd been petting The Great Catsby in the children's section.

"See you Tuesday." Lou waved as the girl skipped over and grabbed her mother's hand.

Hannah crossed the fingers on her free hand. "Let's hope we've got the pet green light from my landlord by then."

Lou smiled. "I'll tell Noah to get the paperwork together just in case." She mirrored Hannah's crossed fingers. Noah, the local veterinarian, assisted Lou in all of the adoptions.

Once they'd gone, Lou stared nostalgically at Catsby. If Tuesday *was* the day, it would be a bittersweet one for Lou. Hannah and her little girl had wanted a cat since they first stepped into Whiskers and Words two months earlier. They'd fallen in love with the sweet black cat. It had taken some convincing, but Hannah just about had her landlord convinced to let them bring a cat into their rental house.

Lou was going to miss the little guy, but she was so excited that he would get a second chance at a family. His first one hadn't gone so well. Apparently, the first little girl who'd owned him didn't want him anymore, and the parents were tired of him clawing up their furniture. Lou had broken him of the scratching within a few days, so she was confident he wouldn't have that issue at his new home.

Hannah and Sage had been in almost daily to spend time with him, and the other cats. Sage and Catsby had bonded almost immediately.

"Must be nice to talk a landlord into anything," Silas grumbled to Catnip Everdeen, who'd wandered back to his lap after his outburst.

Lou's heart ached again at the sight. Silas's retirement home had a strict no-pets policy, so he came and sat here most mornings to get his fix of the cats. Forrest was similarly unable to bring a cat home because his wife was allergic, so he spent breaks there in between clients in the shop. Lou was pretty sure Anne Mice was in love with him. Each time he came in, the beautiful gray cat followed him around until he sat down. Once he had a lap, she was in it.

The rest of the day trotted along sleepily as the cats lounged in the sunbeams and customers wandered through the shop. Monday was more of the same. Lou tried calling Credence a few more times, still without an answer. She closed the shop early that day.

Since she'd opened a couple of months prior, Lou had kept the bookshop open seven days a week. Tourism was too high on the weekends for her to close on Saturday or Sunday, but she was feeling burned out and saw the need for a break. Mondays and Tuesdays were her slowest days, sales wise, so she was trying out closing around noon on those days for the next few weeks.

Once the shop door was locked, Lou contemplated taking a nap—she had a meeting up at the high school in a couple of hours, so she had some time to kill. Instead, she put on her running shoes. It would be good to soak in some of that sunshine. She pulled on a long-sleeve shirt because, even though the sun was shining, there was still a bite to the air.

Lou thought about waiting another day before trying to contact Credence about his book again, but she decided to get it over with today. Grabbing the terrible book from under the register counter, Lou stuffed it in a paper bag—not wanting anyone to see her with such a title. Once outside, she jogged south on Thimble Drive, taking a left on Linen Drive, and a right onto Needle Street. She checked the house numbers until she reached fifteen, the address he'd given her over the phone when he'd used his credit card to pay for the book.

It was a gray house, nothing special—two stories with white trim. Credence's house was, by far, the least exciting house on his block. One house had a veritable forest full of carved wooden creatures set up in the front yard, another held a beautiful pond and fountain, and a garish purple car was parked across the street from his house. Compared to his neighbors, Credence looked like he was making a statement with his sparse yard. The only attempt at a decoration or garden was one sad maple tree right next to the porch.

Catching her breath, Lou jogged up to Credence's front door. She rang the doorbell three times but didn't hear a sound inside. Wondering if the doorbell was broken, Lou rapped her knuckles against the door, trying to be as loud as possible.

The door cracked open a couple of inches from the force of her knock as if the latch hadn't quite clicked into place.

"Hello?" Lou called. When she didn't hear an answer, she peeked through the gap in the door.

Staggering backward, Lou coughed. It smelled awful inside. Prepared for the second time, Lou pulled her shirt up over her nose and approached again.

"Hello?" She pushed the door open a few more inches.

It was just enough to give her a glimpse of the sitting area. But Lou immediately wished she hadn't because sitting in a recliner in the living room was a middle-aged man who'd obviously been dead for a couple of days.

Lou dropped the book she'd been holding and stumbled back. With shaking fingers, she grabbed for her phone and dialed Easton West, a local detective. But before Easton could answer, Lou leaned over the porch and threw up all over the sad little maple tree.

CHAPTER 2

Lou wiped the back of her sleeve along her mouth, her other hand clutching at her stomach. Luckily, she had herself back under control by the time Easton answered his phone.

"Hey, Lou. What's up?" Easton's tone felt entirely too cheerful for what Lou had just experienced. He sounded relaxed, as if he was sitting at his desk at the police station, feet kicked up, gazing out at the beautiful spring day.

"Credence Crowley is dead," she croaked out the sentence.

"What?" Any sense of ease was gone. If Easton had been sitting back, he would've kicked his feet down to the ground and been leaning forward with concern now.

"At least, I think it's him. I've never met him in person." Lou explained how he'd ordered a book over the phone. "I was just stopping by to deliver the book, but the door opened when I knocked, and he's inside. Dead."

"Are you sure? Should I send an ambulance, just in case?" he asked.

Lou paced along the porch. "No. I'm sure. A body doesn't turn

ERYN SCOTT

that color unless ..." She swallowed, the sick feeling returning to her stomach.

"I'm on my way," Easton said. The sound of keys and foot-steps rang through the phone.

Lou hung up and pulled in a deep breath through her nose to quell any more nausea. She was about to move away from the house—and the smell—when she heard a low, loud meow coming from inside.

Her phone conversation with Credence when he'd ordered the book came rushing back to her. He'd mentioned owning a cat.

Oh no. Lou wanted to wait, but the cat's wails grew louder and more desperate. She glanced behind her at the road. No Easton, yet. Lou tugged her long sleeves down over her hands and pulled the collar up over her nose. She elbowed the door open and walked inside. Keeping her eyes forward so she wouldn't have to look at the body again, Lou followed the sounds of desperate meowing. She wandered through a messy kitchen. Old take-out containers littered the countertop, and the cake Hannah had seen Credence buy at the store sat untouched on the counter.

Lou's detail-oriented mind couldn't seem to get past that. He'd bought a birthday cake and hadn't eaten it? Maybe he'd died before he got the chance. Sadness overwhelmed her at the thought.

Locating the source of the meowing, Lou stopped in front of a door next to a stainless-steel refrigerator. There was definitely a cat on the other side of the door. Her heartbeat calmed. It had sounded hurt, but now she knew it was most likely just upset at being confined in the room. The fact that the cat was locked in a room brought forward a list of questions. If Credence had died unexpectedly, why hadn't it been loose in the house?

It was almost as if it had been put in there on purpose, so it wouldn't get near the body.

The thought was chilling enough that as her gaze drifted to the doorknob, Lou found that she couldn't reach forward. She didn't want to ruin anything about the scene by touching the knob. With her shirtsleeves pulled over her hands, she might not add any new fingerprints, but she risked ruining any that were already there.

Lou had read a lot of crime fiction and police procedurals in her time as an editor in New York. In fact, one of her best-selling authors, Olivia Queen, wrote the famous Lily George detective mysteries. Olivia, a retired police officer, would've never put Lily in such a position. Lou backed away, deciding to leave the cat until Easton arrived. The cat's cries still tore at her heart, but she knew help would be there at any moment.

As she walked through the living room again, toward the open front door, she couldn't help but let her focus wander over the scene. She could look away no easier than she'd been able to read through a manuscript without making editing marks and notes in the margins when she was an editor.

Credence, she assumed, sat in a recliner. From the way Silas and the others had described him, Lou had expected the man to be old and crotchety. But he probably hadn't been much older than her. On the side table next to him was a prescription pill bottle and an empty fifth of vodka—the one Hannah had seen him purchasing last week along with the cake, Lou realized. A small, blue shirt button sat on the white pill-bottle top. There was also a piece of paper, folded in half next to that, sitting under the remote control. The scene was so tidy, especially compared to the kitchen.

As Lou scooted by, she couldn't help but notice a bright sparkle on the man's cheek. It was a speck of lime-green glitter. One of the really tiny ones that you could stare straight at, but you don't notice until the light hits it just right.

Odd.

Outside again, Lou poked her head out of her shirt like a turtle coming out of its shell. She gasped, pulling in a deep breath of fresh air as she wiggled her hands out of her long sleeves. The details she'd noticed inside stacked up in her mind like cards in her hand. The only problem was, she wasn't sure what game she was playing, so she didn't know what the cards meant as a group.

She paced on the lawn for a moment before two police cruisers sped down the street, pulling to a stop in Credence's driveway. Easton and three other officers spilled out.

"He's in the living room," Lou said, pointing as she grimaced.

Her frown deepened as the officers stepped over the book she'd dropped on the porch. It had landed with its spine splayed out and pages bent. Oh well, it wasn't a great loss, she decided.

Detective West didn't follow the officers inside, however. He stopped in front of Lou, his expression serious. "Are you okay?"

She set the back of her hand against her forehead. "I'm fine." Her attention turned to the small maple tree next to the porch. "I may have lost my lunch on that tree, though. Sorry."

Easton waved a hand to dismiss her worries. He gestured for her to follow him away from the scene, but she wouldn't budge.

"There's a cat inside. We need to go help it, but I didn't want to ruin anything. It feels like it's a crime scene."

"I'll go inside," Easton said. "Where is it?"

"There's a room off the kitchen. You'll be able to hear it. It's rather upset." Lou twisted her fingers in the fabric of her shirt.

"Would you text Noah and see if he's free? Just in case." Easton's blue eyes seemed to darken as he prepared himself to head inside.

Lou pulled out her phone and sent a message to Noah, the local veterinarian. His clinic should close for the day in about fifteen minutes, so she hoped he would have time to come out. He sent a thumbs-up text back, and Lou breathed out a sigh of relief. He was on his way.

Another cause for relief came when Easton exited the house a moment later, a beautiful tabby in his arms. Both their eyes were wide—the cat's with fear and Easton's with concern. He moved stiffly, like a man who's been handed a baby and doesn't quite know what to do with it.

"I tried to leave it in the room, but it freaked out. It seems happy if I'm holding it," Easton said, discomfort lacing his tone.

Lou held out her hands. "Noah's on his way. I can take it."

The cat's eyes rolled wildly as they made the transfer, but once it was in Lou's arms, it sank into her, settling immediately. A desperate purr rumbled through it as if it were trying to convince itself that everything was okay.

"Poor thing was without food or water in there. I appreciate you preserving the scene, but I don't think you needed to worry about fingerprints," Easton said conversationally as they waited. "It's most likely a suicide, unfortunately." He pressed his mouth into a thin line.

The way he said it so casually made Lou falter for a moment. Sure, the signs were all there. The bottle of pills, the fifth of vodka, no blood or signs of foul play. But to Lou, there had been just as many signs that it couldn't have been suicide. The cap had been screwed back onto the pill bottle, for one, the button sitting neatly on top. Then there was the front door. It hadn't been latched correctly. The cat had been locked inside a room without food or water—or a litter box, Lou guessed. When she'd spoken to Credence on the phone a couple of weeks ago, he'd sounded enamored with his cat. If he were going to kill himself, someone that in love with their pet would've at least set it up with the essentials or let it outside. And then there was the book. Who bought a brand new book with work pages in the back if they planned on killing themself?

Lou shook her head. "That doesn't make sense, Easton. There are too many things that don't add up to a person planning on taking their own life." She described to him all the details she noticed, all the reasons this didn't seem so cut and dried to her.

Easton ran his palm along his clean-shaven chin. "I've seen a lot more suicides than I'd like in my time on the force, Lou. I go through this with the families all the time. They try to nitpick the few things that don't make sense. There are often things that don't add up. The truth is hard to swallow, but it's there. Plus, there was a suicide note, so ..."

Lou gasped, startling the cat in her arms. She apologized, petting it until it calmed. Then she asked, "What did the note say?"

"That's confidential, but believe me, the guy had given up." Easton shot Lou a sidelong glance, making sure she was going to let it drop.

Another car pulled up to the scene; this one was shiny, black, and not a police car. Out stepped a man with silver hair and a tailored gray suit. He wore a serious expression like he'd just come from breaking terrible news to a patient's family.

"That's the medical examiner," Easton said to Lou. "I'd better get going."

Lou's mind raced with possibilities as she held the cat and waited for Noah. She must've been sporting quite the scowl because when Noah pulled up in a truck just a few minutes later, the local veterinarian raced over, obviously assuming the worst.

"What's wrong?" he asked. Running his eyes over the cat, he started his examination before he could even get his hands on it.

Lou softened her face. "Everything's fine—I mean, I think it is —with the cat, anyway." She wrinkled her nose. "Not with Credence."

Her text to him had been vague enough that the poor guy didn't know what he was walking into. Noah's expression flattened.

"Someone finally got him?" he asked.

His cold statement shocked Lou. Noah had been one of the first new friends she'd made in town when she'd moved there two months ago. She'd been drawn to Noah because of his warmth, his kindness, and the way he cared for those around him.

The hostile glower he wore was such a departure from his usual warm, dimpled smile that Lou took a step back.

"Sorry." Noah squeezed his eyes shut for a moment and then opened them again. "I just—the guy was well hated around here and for good reason. He's made everyone's lives as terrible as he can."

Once the shock at Noah's reaction wore off, Lou latched on to the next most interesting thing about what he'd said. "So you assume he was murdered, then?"

"He wasn't?" Noah's eyebrows jumped higher on his forehead. "I just figured…"

Lou wet her lips, looking back at the house while Noah checked the cat's ears, eyes, and gums. "Easton and the other cops seem to think it's suicide."

Noah glanced up from the cat. "But you don't."

She shook her head. "The biggest reason being this little one." She hugged the tabby closer and its purrs increased in volume. "He loved this cat. If he was going to kill himself, don't you think he would've given it to someone to look after, or at least let it outside, not lock it in a room without food, water, or a litter box." Lou snorted.

Noah frowned. "Actually, you've got a point there. Credence was a miserable man, but he loved Jules. That's her name, by the way. He brought her into the clinic for the slightest cold and babied her like a child. You said she was without food or water? I could see him leaving her in a room with plenty of food and water, knowing someone would look for him eventually and find her, but…" Noah scratched at his beard as he thought.

"See?" Lou pushed back her shoulders, feeling vindicated. "Is she okay?"

He nodded. "A little dehydrated and hungry, I'm sure, but we can fix that."

Lou chewed on her lip. "Or I could." When Noah looked up,

she added, "I think Hannah and Sage are going to take Catsby home tomorrow, and we could use someone to fill his space."

Noah finally adopted that signature dimpled smile of his. "I thought you'd be happy to have one less cat to take care of. Sure, if you want to foster her until we get someone to adopt, that would be great." Concern flashed through his brown eyes. "Though I'm not so sure we want to advertise whose cat she was. That could limit the amount of interest she receives."

"Gotcha. Okay, well if there's nothing else for me to do here, I think I'll take her home." Lou glanced back at the house. "I'll text Easton and let him know I'm leaving."

"You two want a ride?" Noah asked, knowing she didn't have a car.

Lou almost laughed at herself for forgetting. "That would be great," she said.

But as Lou climbed into Noah's car, clutching Jules for the short ride back to the bookshop, she definitely didn't feel great. For one, her stomach was still upset—and she was pretty sure she was going to have to bleach her nose to get rid of the memory of that smell. But also because if Easton was treating this like a suicide, that would mean he wouldn't be investigating possible murder suspects. Lou felt it deep in her bones that this was a murder, which meant that if she didn't do something, a killer might walk free.

CHAPTER 3

Jules acclimated quickly to the other felines, a surprise considering she'd been the only cat at Credence's home. Lou had been all prepared to keep her upstairs for a few days, separated from the others, but once she had some water and food, she warmed right up to the other cats.

They got along so well, in fact, that Lou decided Jules was okay to stay out with the rest of the cats while Lou went up to the high school for her appointment.

Lou changed into more professional clothing and then walked up the two blocks to the large brick building. The high school let out at two ten each day, so Lou missed the large exodus of students by arriving at two thirty. Even though most of the students were gone, Lou knew the teachers and staff were contracted to be there at least a half hour after the last bell. Plus, the annual Spring Fling festival was next Friday, and staff was probably staying even later to work on finishing touches.

Especially Lou's best friend, Willow, a horticulture teacher who'd been pressured into coordinating the event.

Lou pulled open the door to the main office. The scent of flowers, popcorn, and stale coffee spilled out to greet her, and Lou guessed the room she could see down the hallway was the teacher's lounge.

She smiled as she stepped up to the front desk. "Hello, Ms. Hovley," Lou said, reading the name tag next to her computer. "I'm here to meet with the librarian, Mrs. Walters. Do I need to sign in?"

The woman behind the desk had a sagging posture and the slack expression of a person who'd been done with the day before breakfast. Her wiry hair flattened to her head in a way that said it was *over it* too. "It's after school hours. Why would you need to sign in?" she asked in a dry monotone.

Lou pressed her lips together and resisted the urge to point to the large sign next to her that said, All Visitors Must Sign In. Questioning the cranky woman probably wouldn't help her mood improve.

"Great." Lou held her chin high in an effort to stay above the woman's bad attitude. "Can you tell me where Willow Grey's classroom is?"

Ms. Hovley narrowed her eyes. "I thought you were going to see the librarian." Suspicion leaked from her pores, and she scanned Lou up and down like she was reconsidering Lou's need to sign in.

"Oh, Willow's my best friend." Lou laughed. "Sorry, that was confusing. I was just going to say hello to her."

Ms. Hovley snorted as if the idea of best friends was just for kids, and adults shouldn't concern themselves with such trivial things. "She's in room two oh three."

Lou almost asked for directions, but she didn't want to spend any more time with the *charming* woman than she had to. That turned out to be a mistake. The school was an absolute maze. Whereas the path to the office had been clearly marked, the rest of the hallways were numbered, none with anything close to 203.

After getting lost three times, Lou finally found Willow's classroom in the science hall. At least, she assumed that was where she was if the posters about cells and elements lining the walls were anything to go on. It made sense that Willow's class would be there. Besides horticulture, she sometimes taught lower-level biology classes.

The door was locked, and the lights were off. Lou frowned but checked her watch. She only would've had a few minutes to chat before her meeting with Mrs. Walters anyway.

Turning back toward the center of the building, Lou located the expansive library with much more ease. She smiled as she pulled in a breath, preparing herself for the meeting. She'd had three similar meetings already last week, one with the public librarian, another with the elementary librarian, and the last with the middle-school librarian. They'd all gone so well that excitement pulsed through Lou as she pushed open the door.

A woman who had to be in her sixties, if not seventies, sat behind the circulation desk. Her long gray hair was braided, the plait thrown over one shoulder. She had a small pair of reading glasses perched on her nose, and she squinted through them at the screen. The familiar beep of books being checked in rang through the place. A large roll of clear tape sat on the counter next to the librarian. She must have been reenforcing book spines earlier in the day.

"Hi, you must be Evelyn Walters," Lou said.

"That's me." The woman looked up from the last book she'd scanned.

"I'm Louisa Henry, the one who emailed you last week." Lou stopped in front of the desk and held out her hand, but the woman held up a right hand encased in a brace.

"I'm sorry, my carpal tunnel is acting up, and if I try to shake your hand, it'll just stay in a claw shape all afternoon." Evelyn checked her watch, giving Lou the impression that she had somewhere to be.

"Oh, I'm sorry," Lou said, cringing. She noticed the librarian was awkwardly using her left—and definitely not her dominant—

hand to check in the books, so it was taking much longer. Getting back on topic, Lou said, "So, like I said in the email, I have some great news to share with you." She pulled in a deep breath, a grin creeping over her face. "Well, you see … I've recently sold a very expensive first edition. It wasn't really mine, even though it was in my shop."

Noticing the woman was checking the clock yet again, Lou tried to skip ahead, thinking through the rest of the story: finding the book hidden in her shop, Easton insisting she keep it, her feeling that she shouldn't, and finally her decision to sell the book and donate the proceeds to the local libraries. Evelyn didn't need to know about any of that.

Skipping to the end, Lou said, "So each school and the local library will get fifteen thousand dollars for books." She lifted her shoulders in celebration, waiting for the laughing, hugging, and celebrating that had happened with the other three librarians.

"Wow. Fifteen thousand?" Evelyn forced a smile, but Lou didn't miss the frantic look of panic that crossed her features for the split second before. "Okay. Right. I can handle that." The librarian seemed to talk to herself, like she was trying to convince herself this was a good thing.

The woman's reaction felt like a slap to the face, and Lou had to try hard not to take a step back in surprise.

Lou cleared her throat. "Is everything okay?" she asked.

Evelyn's worried expression softened. "Oh, I'm sorry. It's just, I'm retiring in a few months, my daughter just moved in with me along with her three teenage children, I already have surgery scheduled for this darn hand but now my knee is acting up. I thought I could make it until the summer before I needed surgery, but I don't know if I can wait. And unlike my carpal tunnel surgery, this knee is going to take a lot longer to heal." Again, Evelyn gave Lou one of those unconvincing smiles as she gestured to her left knee.

Lou's eyes went wide. "Oh, that's a lot."

Evelyn waved her hands in the air dismissively. "I'm happy to do it, of course. I love my grandkids, and spending time with them is even more important after what happened to their father." Evelyn's expression fell as she whispered, "Hit by a drunk driver," as if they were in the room and she didn't want them to hear.

Lou's heart went out to Evelyn's daughter and her grandkids. Lou knew how much it hurt to lose a husband. She couldn't imagine what the kids were going through, losing their father.

Evelyn placed a hand on her forehead. "It's just that my daughter works full time, and I'm trying to help her with all the picking up and dropping off that needs to happen. I'm running around a lot and have less time to catch up on stuff around here." She puffed out an exhale as she looked at the stacks of books. "Which I desperately need to do because this darn hand is slowing me down." She waved a hand at Lou so she wouldn't worry about her. "So fifteen thousand? That's a lot of books." Evelyn tried to sound enthusiastic.

"I could help with the ordering," Lou offered, realizing this would be just one more thing on Evelyn's already full plate.

The older woman clasped her hands to her chest. "That would be so lovely of you. Are you sure you have time?"

Lou nodded. With her closing the shop early two days a week, she would definitely have extra time to help. Plus, how much time could ordering books take?

In answer to Lou's unspoken question, Evelyn added, "We got a big donation of used books last month that I still haven't gone through, so you'll probably want to start there to make sure you don't get doubles." Evelyn cringed, realizing how much time that was adding to the favor.

But Lou gave her a crisp nod, trying not to show any doubt. "That's okay. I can help with that too."

Evelyn grasped at Lou's hand with her left one. "Oh, thank you. That's so amazing." She checked her watch again. "I have to go. The youngest has ballet lessons." She swiped her purse from under the counter and gestured toward the desk. "Use anything you need," she said over her shoulder as she scurried out the door.

Lou stood there alone for a moment in shock, unsure where to start. When the door swung open, a relieved smile played at the corners of Lou's mouth. She turned, expecting to see Evelyn come back inside with more directions.

But it wasn't Mrs. Walters.

"Lou, what are you doing standing in the library alone?" Willow cocked her head to the side.

Lou stretched her arms out wide before letting them fall. "I'm not entirely sure what just happened, actually." She recounted her conversation with the busy librarian and the cranky secretary before that.

Willow widened her eyes. "Yikes. Between her and Mary at the front desk, it sounds like you haven't gotten the best impression of the school. Sorry. Evelyn really is lovely, it's just, her daughter's life kind of imploded once she lost her husband, and Evelyn's only holding on by a thread until she can retire. Mary is another issue altogether," Willow scoffed. "I'm not sure how she keeps her job. Everyone thinks it's because she was Flora's neighbor growing up, so she has a soft spot for the grouch." Willow blinked, seeming to remember why Lou was there. "I'm sorry you got roped into extra work, though."

"It's fine," Lou said, the oddness of her meeting slowly fading away. "I'm happy to help. Picking out books will be fun. You can help me decide what the high schoolers like to read."

It was with that comment that Lou noticed Willow's normally rosy cheeks were pale and her bright blue eyes dim with fatigue. The last time Lou had seen her friend looking so poorly was when Willow had found out her fiancé was cheating on her.

"Honest three," Lou said, crossing her arms.

Willow's face crumpled for a moment at hearing her friend's

prompt for an emotional check-in, but she pulled in a deep breath and said, "Overwhelmed. Tired. Stressed. This Spring Fling festival is a lot of work."

Lou had guessed as much from her friend's appearance but was glad she'd asked. "How about this? I could help you with the festival," Lou amended, realizing that Willow didn't have the time or energy to help with ordering books.

Willow sighed. "Or we could both help each other. Sorry, I'm just swamped. This is why no one else signed up to be the coordinator, I'm realizing."

Lou wrapped an arm around her friend. "I can definitely help. It sounds like I'll need to be here a lot in my spare time anyway to go through books before I can even start the ordering."

"Thanks," Willow said as they walked down the hall. "How was your day? Did Hannah and Sage take Catsby home?" Excitement lit up her expression.

Lou shook her head. "Tomorrow. I'm going to miss him so much. But ..." she dragged out the word. "I've already replaced him with another friend," Lou admitted.

Willow laughed. "Where'd you find another cat so soon?"

At this, Lou's grimace deepened. "That's a much longer story."

Willow motioned for Lou to follow her down the hall. She pulled out a ring of keys and stopped in front of the same classroom the woman at the front desk had directed Lou to. It wasn't until they arrived that Lou realized she'd failed to pay attention to the route Willow had taken. Lou feared she was sure to get lost again the next time she tried to locate her friend's classroom.

Unlocking the room, Willow held the door, ushering Lou inside. Lou had visited Willow in Button many times over the last decade. It was on the first of such trips that she'd set foot in Button Books—the former name of Whiskers and Words. But whenever Lou was visiting, she and Willow spent time at Willow's home or drove south to Seattle for a bit of city fun. She'd never seen Willow's classroom or the greenhouse between the school building and the large football field and track. Similarly, Lou had never brought Willow to the publishing house offices in all the times she'd flown out to visit Lou in New York. It was fun to be able to share in their work lives now that they lived in the same town.

Willow's classroom was huge. It held workstations for groups of students to sit around and work collaboratively on projects or listen to instruction. In the corner, her teacher desk was piled with a dozen different potted plants. Pictures covered the wall behind her desk. Most of them featured OC, Willow's large chestnut horse. And there were many of Willow and Lou throughout the years. One of them in middle school, when they'd gone through their big hair phase. Them graduating high school together. Standing with the Statue of Liberty in the background on Willow's first trip to visit Lou in New York when they'd still been in college. Willow standing with Lou at her wedding.

There were a lot of opportunities for pictures when you met your best friend when you were seven.

A few of the pictures featured Lou and her late husband, Ben. Lou walked forward, her fingers touching the edges of the photographs. She missed him so much it hurt. His smile could brighten even the rainiest of New York days. His laugh could pull her out of even the worst moods. Ben's bright eyes and dark beard were so familiar to her, yet after almost a year, the fear that he was disappearing from her memory gripped at her chest sometimes, like she'd swallowed a piece of ice.

Willow came up beside Lou and wrapped an arm around her shoulder. "So tell me about this new cat," she said. Motioning for Lou to sit in her desk chair, Willow pulled herself up onto one of the student workstations, sitting on top in a way Lou was sure she didn't allow her students to do.

"Do you know Credence Crowley?" Lou asked.

Willow rolled her eyes. "Unfortunately. My car needed some work last year."

Inhaling, Lou said, "Well, I stopped by his house today to drop off a book he ordered, and …" She swallowed, her throat growing hot and metallic at the memory. "He was dead."

Willow gasped, her hand flying to cover her open mouth. "Oh man. That's awful. How did he die?"

Lou folded her hands in her lap. "Easton's sure it's suicide, but—"

"You're not so convinced," Willow interrupted.

"Sour people like Credence don't have enough empathy to blame themself for anything wrong in their life. I'm not saying those kinds of people never die by suicide, but it feels wrong," Lou said. She explained the other things about the scene that just didn't make sense.

"Easton should know better than to discount your attention for detail after what happened a couple of months ago." Willow clicked her tongue. "His loss."

Lou shrugged. "Maybe."

"Don't pretend with me," Willow said, pointing a finger at Lou. "I know that look in your eyes. Detective Lou is definitely on the case."

CHAPTER 4

The next morning, Lou said goodbye to The Great Catsby. Hannah and Sage showed up with the paperwork from Noah for the adoption right when she opened. It was another sunny day, and the cats lazed about in the beams, tails or ears flicking every so often. Jules had taken to the cat bed set up next to the front window, and she stretched out as the warm sun bathed her furry belly.

The Japanese magnolia trees that had been outside Lou's front windows for the past couple of months were gone, moved back to the high school to be tended by Willow's horticulture students. And while the lack of leaves impeding the windows definitely let more light through, Lou missed the dappled, green-tinted patterns they used to create on the floor. She would have to ask her friend about purchasing replacements for the trees.

The only cloud hanging over the otherwise perfect morning was Purrt. Despite the pleasant introductions the day before, Purrt seemed to have developed a problem with the new arrival. He had yet to hiss at Jules but followed her around, finding a place to perch about a yard away from wherever she was so he could glare at the tabby. Jules seemed none the wiser to his hatred, however, and Lou figured he'd get over it soon.

She got to work tidying shelves, petting cats, and making a large cup of coffee. Despite all the good surrounding her, she couldn't keep her thoughts from sliding back to the terrible scene she'd witnessed at Credence's house.

Lou had initially shrugged off Willow's Detective Lou comment from yesterday, but her curiosity had only increased in the hours in between then and now. If no one else was going to investigate Credence's death, she felt responsible for doing at least a little digging. She hadn't known Credence, but he hadn't seemed as terrible as everyone made him out to be when she'd talked to him on the phone. Mostly, Lou didn't want a killer out there, loose in the town.

But if he really had been murdered, who should she look into first? Who could've done it? Her mind latched on to the tired father, Timothy, who'd visited her shop Sunday. The regulars had mentioned that Timothy had a recent run-in with Credence. They'd talked about how much he'd hated Credence. Lou wondered if it was enough to kill him.

Lou was chewing on her lip, deep in thought, when Silas showed up for the day.

He let out a whoosh of air as he settled into the armchair. "Quite the scene you must've stumbled upon yesterday," he said. "Can't say I didn't warn you not to go looking for him, though." Silas didn't make eye contact, instead staring at his paper. He often spoke to her like this, as if it were less personal if he pretended to be doing something else at the same time.

Lou leaned her elbows on the checkout counter. "It was pretty awful." She ran her finger along the edge of the computer, checking for dust. "Say, Silas. You don't know what happened between Timothy and Credence, do you?"

Silas's fluffy gray eyebrows lifted as he looked up from his newspaper. "I do."

Lou bit back a smile as she realized he wouldn't give her information so easily. "Was it bad?"

He puffed out his cheeks. "'Bout as bad as they come."

He shuffled his newspaper, and Lou thought for a moment that he was going to go back to reading it. But Silas finally folded it and turned his attention toward her.

"Timothy had a trip planned to go down to California for a family reunion. He'd been blabbing on about it for weeks. It would've been the first time many of his relatives were going to get to meet the triplets." Catnip Everdeen must've heard Silas's voice, because as he told the story, she trotted over and vaulted up into his lap. He let his hand slide absentmindedly over her fur as he talked. "The morning they were supposed to leave, that dang van of theirs wouldn't start. He goes to Credence to see if he'll come check it out. The sleaze said he would, but for triple his regular rate."

Lou's mouth parted in surprise. "Did he know it was an emergency?"

"Why do you think he knew he could get away with that?" Silas sent a pointed look her way.

"Couldn't Timothy have taken it somewhere else?" Lou asked.

Silas tapped the tip of his nose. "That's Credence's superpower. Or, it was, anyway." The old man frowned. "He ran any other repair shops out of town, so he's the only one for an hour. Unless people want to pay to have their car towed thirty miles to Kirk, they're stuck using him."

Lou shook her head. "You're making me want to stay car free for longer, if I can help it."

There hadn't ever been a need for a car in New York City, and Lou had yet to check that off her to-do list out here.

"Exactly my sentiment," said Silas, crossing his arms and puffing out his chest, pretending his lack of a car was by choice instead of because his license had been revoked when he'd hit a post office box last year—according to Willow. Silas's assisted-living apartment complex was up on Thimble Drive, though, so he could easily walk most places he needed to go.

"So Timothy paid the ridiculous price?" Lou asked.

Silas uncrossed his arms. "He did. Credence said it was the timing belt that had snapped. He installed a new one, took the van on a quick test drive to make sure it worked, and they were off to California."

Wrinkling her nose, Lou contemplated that. It didn't make Credence look good at all. But it also didn't seem like a motive for murder.

"Oh, that's just the start of it." Silas must've recognized the doubt in her expression. "The Davis family didn't make it very far before the engine seized. A mechanic down south a ways told them there wasn't a drop of oil in the thing. Now, seeing as how Timothy had just checked the oil himself the day before, he knew that wasn't true. But he couldn't prove it was Credence who'd tampered with it, even though it probably was."

"Why would Credence drain his oil?" Lou asked in shock.

"Probably thought Timothy would notice the oil light and bring it back," Silas said. "It would mean more money in Credence's pocket if he could up-charge him on that too. The problem was Timothy didn't notice the light until it was too late, probably got distracted by crying babies and such."

"So they didn't make it to the reunion?" Lou asked, crestfallen for Timothy and his family.

Silas's posture slumped. "They did not. They were so tired and still had too long to travel. All the money he had to put into the repairs meant they couldn't afford a rental car *and* the trip down there anymore. So they came back."

"And Credence denied touching the oil?" Lou guessed, sure the answer was going to be yes.

"He has a sign posted in his garage that says, No Free Inspections. He doesn't touch your oil or any of the fluids unless you pay him to, and a timing belt wouldn't call for him to get near the oil pan."

"But he obviously did this time," Lou said just as the door opened and Forrest walked inside. "Maybe he messed with the oil when he took it on the test drive. Hi, Forrest." Lou smiled.

Silas waved a hello to Forrest and said, "Who knows. Timothy sure believed Credence did. He said he topped off with oil he already had at home, so there wasn't a receipt proving he'd bought any. A few locals think he must've overlooked adding oil in his tired state, but ..." Silas left it at that, knowing there wasn't a way to figure out the truth now that Credence was dead.

"Poor Timothy," Forrest said, jumping right into the conversation. "I've had three people tell me I need to schedule an appointment with him so he can talk through his frustration instead of driving by Credence's house all slow and menacingly at two in the morning."

"Two in the morning?" Lou asked, surprised.

"One of his girls doesn't sleep well and putting her in the car does the trick. Grace, I think it is?" Forrest tipped his head to the side. "But now I guess it doesn't matter."

Lou leaned forward on the register counter. "I guess," she said, not convinced it didn't.

"We all thought he sauntered through life being awful to everyone around him and letting everything run off his back. But it seems like it really affected him after all." Forrest rubbed a hand over his beard.

Lou knew she should probably drop it, but she had a psychologist here, and she didn't want to lose the chance to pick his brain about the doubts running through her mind.

"Are you sure? I didn't know him well, but from everyone's stories, I get the sense that he couldn't have cared less that everyone hated him." Lou gauged Forrest's reaction.

Forrest exhaled. "The one thing I've learned from my years inside people's heads is that people surprise you."

Lou tapped her fingers on the counter. He wasn't wrong. But something she'd learned in her almost forty years on the planet was that people were simple. Not in a mean way, like they were stupid, but that their actions were often more predictable because they were motivated by the same raw emotions and fears.

"And who is this?" Forrest's tone dropped into an even more velvety register than it usually was as he noticed the tabby cat strutting toward him. Forrest looked up at Lou. "Catsby gone?"

Lou nodded.

"And you've replaced him already?" Silas snorted, shoving his hands into a crossed posture.

"It just happened," Lou said, deciding Noah was right about keeping the identity of this cat's former owner a secret. They didn't seem to know that Credence had even had a cat, and she wasn't going to be the one to tell them. "This is Jules Purrne."

Forrest chuckled as he leaned down to pet the gorgeous tabby. "Jules Verne. I get it."

Lou had really liked the name Jules, but all of her fosters got fancy new literary-themed names to help with their adoption. And even though Jules Verne was a male author, Lou liked the idea of the cat keeping the same first name. She made a note to type up an adoption sheet for the newest cat. Catsby's had gone home with Hannah and Sage in their adoption packet.

"What does Timothy Davis do?" Lou asked, hoping her transition back to Credence's death wasn't too obvious.

"He stays home with the girls," Silas said. "His wife is a high-powered lawyer in Kirk, and he loves being with those triplets, so it all worked out."

Apparently, deciding the conversation was over, Silas picked up his newspaper again. Forrest cracked open the book he'd brought with him. Lou used the silence to contemplate her next steps. If she wanted to talk to Timothy, she would either have to wait until he came into the shop again, hope she ran into him around town, or figure out where he lived.

Thanking her past self for not throwing out the phone book that had been under the checkout counter when she'd first arrived in the shop, Lou hoped she would find an address in there for Timothy Davis.

THAT AFTERNOON, she closed the shop at two and headed out on a walk. She clutched two books in her hand as she walked. A piece of paper with an address on it stuck out from in between the books—the Davis's address.

The Davis family lived in the Forest Pond neighborhood off Pin Street. It was a cute development with cheerfully colorful houses in rows, but it wasn't overcrowded as many such neighborhoods can be. Each home had a large backyard with forest behind it, complete with a communal pond.

From Thread Lane, Lou took a left onto Pin Street and into the neighborhood. She pulled out the paper again, but didn't really need to check because she'd memorized the address: 324 Pin Street.

The house was a buttercream yellow that made warmth radiate through Lou just looking at it. She gripped the books tighter as she jogged up to the front door. She had her story all straight and hoped it would get her the answers to a few questions.

The porch held two rocking chairs, and Lou hoped they could speak outside since—if Timothy really was responsible for Credence's death—she didn't want to be alone inside with him. She'd also texted her plan to Willow, who was still at the school, but said she would drive over there frantically if she didn't hear from Lou in five minutes.

Sending the thumbs-up emoji to her friend as she said she would right before knocking, Lou gently tapped her knuckles against the door.

While she and Ben hadn't been able to have children, Ben's brother had given them two amazing nieces, and she'd vicariously experienced the agony of trying to keep a sleeping baby down, especially when there was more than one little one in the house.

Lou was about to knock again, not sure if she'd been loud enough the first time. But before she could, the door swung open. Timothy stood before her, just as rumpled in appearance as he'd been in the bookshop the other day, when he'd been searching for the book she held two more copies of in her hand.

He pointed to a video doorbell. "Sorry if I startled you. I try to catch people before they knock." He scooted out toward her, clutching a baby monitor in his hands. "All three are asleep at once, which is some sort of miracle and I don't want to mess it up."

"Oh, sure." Lou lowered her voice to a whisper to match Timothy's. "Sorry to bother you. I own the bookstore you were at the other day."

Timothy's expression dropped. He patted his pockets. "Oh no. Did I leave my credit card there? Why does this always happen to m—"

"No, nothing like that." Lou interrupted him. "I heard you have triplets, and I thought I would bring over two more copies of the book they love so much. You know, in case it's misplaced again. This way they can all have their own copy." She held the books forward.

The tired man's eyes crowded with tears as if this was the nicest thing to happen to him all year. "Thank you. That's so lovely. I…" And then he was crying. "I'm sorry." He swiped at his misty eyes. "I really love being home with them, but I'm just exhausted. It has to get easier, right?"

Lou wet her lips. "I don't have any kids, so I wouldn't be able to tell you for sure, but it has to. Or else why do people keep having them, right?"

He sniffled, holding up the books. "Thank you so much. It's a lovely gift."

Lou smiled and surveyed the neighborhood. She thought about how she might slip in her questions about Credence, how she might get him to confess a motive or opportunity for the murder. But the longer she sat here with this man, cradling a monitor that showed his three adorable daughters sleeping soundly, it felt increasingly silly to think he had anything to do with what happened to Credence Crowley.

Timothy glanced at his hands uncomfortably.

"Okay, well," Lou said, placing her hands on her knees. "I'll let you get back inside to the girls. I hope they continue to enjoy that book. I can't wait for them to come into the shop when they're older."

"If my wife and I have any say in it, they're going to be big readers." Timothy's eyes lit up as he talked about his daughters. He waved goodbye.

As she jogged away from the Davis house, Lou knew she'd made the right decision by dropping the idea of interrogating Timothy. The only problem was she didn't know who to look into next or whether she should keep investigating at all.

CHAPTER 5

L ou's mind buzzed with thoughts of the case as she jogged back home from the Davis residence, just as it had on the way there. Unlike before, however, her thoughts turned to worries such as *I need to focus on my business* and *Why am I getting involved in another murder investigation?*

Those anxious thoughts were momentarily interrupted as she approached the enormous decrepit mansion sitting on the plot of land in between Pattern Drive, Pin Street, and Thread Lane.

Each time she passed by the huge house on her daily runs, questions crowded her mind. It was the largest single dwelling she'd seen in Button, which was filled with primarily cute cottages and ramblers. This behemoth probably held at least ten bedrooms within, but it was falling apart. Its brown exterior paint had peeled off in long strips, the multipeaked roof was covered in moss, and some of the windows held plywood boards instead of glass. Huge stalks of overgrown bamboo shielded it from the road, making it appear like a child hiding during a game of hide-and-seek. Small Christmas-tree-like firs hemmed in the house on all other sides.

The last few times she'd run by, Lou had assumed the place

39

was deserted, but today there was a new potted lily sitting just outside the front door. Lou slowed even more, but she didn't want to seem like she was lurking, so she picked up her pace again.

Once she passed the mystery mansion, she let her mind return to Credence's possible murder. She'd been more or less dragged into trouble the last time she'd gotten involved with a murder investigation. She didn't *have* to put herself into trouble this time. Besides, it was a good bet that the people who'd known Credence his whole life had a better read on him than Lou did. Maybe he had genuinely killed himself. Lou could admit she was wrong and move on.

Arriving back at the bookshop only cemented her need to take a step back from the case. Through the large front windows, a few of the cats were visible. Lou's cat, Sapphire, a deaf white cat, napped on a stack of books in the window. He blinked open a single jewel-toned blue eye, probably feeling her blocking his warm sun. She smiled and blew him a kiss before he went back to sleep.

Lou had a wonderful little world here, and she needed to give it the time and devotion it deserved. Plus, she had a lot going on with helping order books for the high school library and helping her best friend plan this Spring Fling celebration—something she was going to do right now, come to think of it.

Lou regarded the running clothes she wore, wondering if she should change, but she figured that festival prep might be sweaty or dirty work, so she just went with what she had on.

She rounded the corner of the bookshop and walked up Thimble Drive toward the high school. Entering the school this time, Lou didn't bother going into the office. Her last encounter with Mary Hovley had made her less than inclined to repeat the experience, and Mary had made it clear that she didn't need to sign in after school hours.

Skipping the office, however, meant that even if Lou remembered any of her roundabout route from the first day, today was all new. She got lost four times before she finally found herself in the science hall, standing in front of Willow's classroom. This time the light was on inside and the door open.

"Knock knock," Lou said, rapping her knuckles against the wall.

Inside, Lou found Willow sitting in a pile of crêpe paper, tissue paper, construction paper, and glitter. Lou laughed, covering her mouth with her hand when Willow scowled up at her.

"I'm sorry, you just look—"

"Ridiculous?" Willow guessed, groaning and pulling herself up off the floor. "I'm not a party planner. I hate this. I'm learning that everyone has high expectations for this event."

"Spring Fling is a big deal around here, huh?" Lou asked, plucking a piece of crêpe paper from Willow's shoulder.

Willow dusted the last bit of glitter off her hands. "I just got done being lectured by your *best friend* about how I'd better not ruin the festival's great reputation."

Lou squinted. "Mary?"

Willow sighed. "Yep. She's being super intense about it, sure I'm going to mess it up."

Grabbing a whiteboard marker from the tray at the front of the room, Lou said, "Well, then let's make sure it's perfect. What needs to be done?"

"Okay, I've got the list of vendors and booths," Willow said, "but I need to check with the students on the festival committee to find out if they've done their last confirmations, and I still need to make a master schedule."

Lou jotted down those jobs.

"Decorations are in progress, but I can't find out what all needs to be decorated. I can't seem to remember from previous years. It's like I wore blinders because it didn't have to do with me." She scratched at her head.

Lou wrote *Decorations? How many?* "Is there a different theme each year, or is it always the same?" she asked.

ERYN SCOTT

"Spring flowers, green, hope. That kind of thing." Willow tiredly waved a hand toward Lou. Her tone was anything but hopeful.

Lou smiled. "I'm wondering if they ever have decorations left over that they reuse from year to year, so you don't have to recreate the whole flower wheel, you know? Who was the chairperson last year?"

Willow scrunched her nose. "Mary. She's done it every year I've been here. Why do you think I was talking to her in the first place? She won't tell me anything helpful, though, and each time I go ask her, it turns into a lecture."

"Why isn't she chairing this year if she has so many opinions?" Lou asked.

"She said she had something else going on that was going to take a lot of her time and focus, so she couldn't." Willow let her shoulders lift and then fall.

Lou sucked in a deep breath. "Okay, maybe we could go snooping around the building. They've been doing this for ages, right? There have to be pictures."

Willow snapped her fingers. "There's a two-page spread on the event in the yearbook." She moved to the other side of the room. "I saw some old yearbooks around here the other day. I think the yearbook class used to meet in here before I was hired." Willow approached a tall cabinet at the back of her classroom. "They were in here somewhere …" She pulled out a stack of textbooks and set it all on the workstation behind her.

Lou was about to suggest they ask about yearbooks in the office—maybe they would know where they keep the old ones— when Willow said, "Ta-da!" and produced an armful of yearbooks. "It's a random compilation of years, but it'll be a good start."

Setting them on the workstation, Willow took the one on top and flipped it open. Lou grabbed the next one on the pile.

"We always hold Spring Fling outside on the track and field

42

unless it's raining, like it obviously was this year." Willow pointed to the pictures in the yearbook in front of her, which were all inside the high school commons, unlike the ones in the yearbook in front of Lou, which were outside.

"This long vine and some flowers are reused from year to year," Lou said, pointing to a large decoration that showed up in both of their yearbooks even though they were five years apart.

Willow chewed on her lip. "Yeah, but these are from at least ten years ago. I wonder if it's still around."

Lou grabbed another yearbook, that one from exactly twenty years ago. She flipped it open.

Her eyes went wide as she found the Spring Fling pages. "Noah was Spring King?" She gawked at a picture of a young Noah Ramero standing onstage wearing a red velvet cape and crown. She also recognized Cassidy French, Noah's ex-wife, standing next to him.

Willow chuckled. "Yes, he and Cassidy are coming back for the twenty-year celebration. It's tradition around here that they run the cakewalk station. They did for their ten-year too."

"I didn't realize he and Cassidy were high school sweet-hearts," Lou said. "That's cute."

Willow rolled her eyes. "I know."

"They seem to get along better than any divorced couple I know," Lou said. "Why'd they split?"

"Cassidy left Noah for some real estate guy she met at a conference in Seattle." Willow's eyes widened. "She claimed she never cheated, but it was a kick in the gut for Noah for sure. And don't let them fool you. They haven't always been this civil." Willow shook her head. "The first few months after the divorce were brutal. The town tried to take sides. Cassidy tried to avoid Noah. But they both love Marigold and saw it was affecting her. Noah told me once that she's more important than any of his anger toward Cassidy, so he forgave her and is trying to move on.

Plus, I think they're way more cooperative as divorced people than they ever were married."

Willow came over and stood behind Lou, peering over her shoulder at the picture of Noah and Cassidy as Spring Fling king and queen.

"Wait … if this was Noah's senior year…" Willow said, flipping back through the pages of the yearbook until small student pictures filled the page. She let out a loud laugh as she pointed to Easton West.

The boy in the picture still looked like Easton, but he'd definitely filled out in the last twenty years.

"He looks so gangly." Willow cackled.

"He and Noah were in the same grade?" Lou asked.

"No. Easton was a junior when Noah was a senior." Willow pointed to the different headings at the top of the pages with their pictures on them. "With as goofy as he looked, he was still the captain of the basketball team, though. Good for Easton." Willow let a small smile curl across her lips.

Lou watched her friend. It was times like this that she realized Willow might not hate her neighbor as much as she claimed to. But Lou wasn't going to push it.

Flipping back to the Spring Fling pages, Lou started making a list. "Okay, there are paper flowers everywhere." She pointed to large flowers made of construction paper. "And these vines could be made by crumpling up long strips of the same type of paper."

Willow nodded. "The art teacher has some of those big rolls of paper in her classroom. I can get the kids to work on those during our planning meeting tomorrow."

"First, let's go search and see if there are any left over from last year. I'd hate for them to do all the work when we don't have to." Lou got to her feet.

They toured the high school, Willow giving a verbal history of each space as they scoured the closets and storage rooms. Lou loved exploring the old building.

The scents of dusty brick, old textbooks, and floor wax surrounded them as they walked into each space. It was the type of school that would've known the scent of chalkboard erasers and white dust floating through the air so many years ago. The hallways were clean and well taken care of, but there wasn't much that could be done to cover the signs of age evident in every corner of the building. Decades of painting over the old brick had it made it so the indentation from the grout was almost gone. The laminate flooring sorely needed a waxing and refinishing.

The pictures hanging on the gym wall of the various sports teams and their trophies dated back to before Lou's parents were born, telling a story of a building with significant history.

"The gym is actually the newest section of the school. It was built during the seventies, but they built everything else back at the start of the Cold War, I think," Willow explained as they finished checking the equipment room and turned back toward the main building.

"That old?" Lou asked, puffing out her cheeks.

Willow's shoulders pushed back with pride. "It's a pretty cool building because of that. There are a few civil defense shelters hidden inside, though I've only seen one." She pointed to a pathway. "This is the auditorium. It's got a cool old sound booth behind the seats."

Lou studied the space in awe as they entered, the smell of dusty curtains and old fabric thick in the large room. Willow flipped on the first bank of lights and motioned to a door off to the right of the stage. "That's where they store the props from plays, and the last place I think the Spring Fling decorations might be."

They checked the storage room. It held old props and costumes from productions throughout the years. Just when they were about to give up, Lou investigated a bright spot of green in the corner. She moved aside the front section of a pirate ship and found a pile of paper flowers and vines.

"I found them!" she called to Willow, who was extricating herself from a wooden taxicab prop on the other side of the space.

"Oh, this is perfect. Now that we have these samples, I can have the decorating committee work on making more tomorrow." She gathered as many as she could in her arms and Lou took the rest. "Thank you."

"No problem," Lou said as they headed back to the main building.

Lou's mind whirred with questions now that she knew more about the building's history. She wondered what other secrets hid within its walls.

A crudely carved set of initials on one of the locker doors caught Lou's eye as they walked back to Willow's classroom, paper flowers clutched in their arms. The letters were C.C., and Lou couldn't help but think of Credence Crowley. The reminder brought to light the fact that Noah and Easton weren't the only ones who'd gone to Button High when they were younger.

And if Noah had been Spring King and Easton the captain of the basketball team, what had Credence's legacy been in these dusty halls?

CHAPTER 6

Lou and Willow had just gotten back to the classroom and had deposited the Spring Fling decoration samples into an enormous pile when Willow's phone rang.

Willow flinched when she looked down at the screen. "Hey, Easton. What's up?" she asked, sandwiching her phone between her ear and her shoulder. A groan escaped her. "Again? Okay, I'll be right there to grab him. Sorry."

Lou didn't need to hear Easton's part of the conversation to know that Willow's horse, OC, must've escaped. He was a master of breaking out of his paddock and making a beeline for Easton's extensive vegetable garden next door. OC was short for Of Course, as in the line from the *Mr. Ed* theme song. But lately, his name seemed to stand for an answer to the question, "Will the horse cause trouble?"

Hanging up, Willow grimaced. "I think we're going to have to call it a day," she said.

"We could take some of this back to your place if you want to keep planning," Lou suggested.

Willow's posture relaxed. "That would be amazing. We could do a working dinner if you don't have other plans."

Lou's other plans were to curl up with a book and the cats and reheat a slice of quiche she'd bought the day before. Dinner with her best friend sounded like a wonderful alternative, even if it did include corralling a mischievous horse and working more on Spring Fling planning.

They drove out to Willow's little farmhouse, a pacing Easton in the front yard when they pulled up.

"What did he get today?" Willow asked, a frown marring her features as she walked up to him.

The tall detective sighed. "Well, let's just say, I won't be making any zucchini bread for a few weeks."

Willow pinched the bridge of her nose. "Easton, I'm so sorry."

Their amicable attitudes surprised Lou. Usually the two neighbors were downright contentious with each other, but Willow seemed genuinely sorry, and Easton was even smiling.

Surprising her even more, Easton laughed. "You know what? It's not so bad. He actually came right up to me when I got home. He had half a zucchini in his mouth, but he trotted over and let me lead him back to the paddock."

Willow's eyes widened. "You're kidding."

Lou knew from chats on the phone with Willow over the years that part of Easton's frustration with OC was that, not only did he have an affinity for Easton's homegrown vegetables, but he also ran from Easton like they were in some kind of forced game of tag.

Worry clouded Easton's expression as he added, "I'm worried his cooperation might've been because he got a pretty nasty cut on his front leg busting through the fence, though. I called Noah; I hope that's okay."

"That's perfect. Thank you." But Willow's body language had significantly stiffened at the mention of an injury.

"Should we go check on him?" Lou suggested, to which Willow added a thankful smile.

"Please," she said with a nervous laugh.

"For the first time in a while, Steve was actually not part of the breakout attempt," Easton explained as they walked around back to where the paddocks and Willow's outdoor arena were.

Steve, Willow's goat, had been purchased as a companion in the hope that being less lonely would help OC care less about escaping. As it turned out, Steve was almost *more* mischievous than his larger counterpart.

"That's surprising," Willow said with a snort. "Did you know that little goat found his way inside my house the other day?" She chuckled. "I must've left the sliding door slightly cracked, off the porch, and I was making dinner when he just waltzed up to me, like 'what are we having?'"

They laughed at the mental image. It was then that Easton noticed the yearbooks Lou clutched.

"Oh man, what do you have these for?" he asked, reading the year stamped on the front of the volume closest to him.

Lou handed the yearbook over to him. "Willow's in charge of the festival this year, and Mary's not exactly being helpful in the planning or decorations department, so we thought we'd look through past yearbooks for ideas about how to decorate."

Easton's eyes lit up. "I could help. You know, I went to high school there and took part in my fair share of Spring Flings."

"Oh, we know. We saw your picture." Willow giggled as they tromped through her backyard.

"Careful what you say; he just volunteered to help. You don't want him to take that back." Lou shot her friend a warning look.

Easton pointed at Lou. "Yeah, listen to her. Plus, I couldn't help what size my ears were at that age."

Willow smiled back at them, but Lou could tell she wouldn't be calm until she confirmed OC was okay.

The large horse was in the paddock as they walked back. The broken fence board sat diagonally across the opening to keep him contained. When OC noticed Willow, he nickered and threw his head, so it almost looked like he was telling her to hurry and come over.

"I just propped up the broken fence piece," Easton explained. "He didn't seem to want to try hopping over it. Again, another reason I thought he might not be feeling well."

Willow closed the distance with a jog. "Hey, Troublemaker."

OC trotted over to the fence just as Willow arrived.

"Oh, you're fine." She scratched under his forelock and tapped him lovingly on the nose. "You had me scared there, big guy."

Lou and Easton stayed back a bit to give Willow and her horse some space. Lou could've sworn she saw Easton's lips arch slightly as he watched Willow with OC. It only added to the anecdotal proof Lou was gathering in her mind that Easton didn't hate her or her horse as much as he pretended to.

Before Lou and Easton could join Willow, Noah walked up, stopping beside them.

"He doesn't look maimed beyond repair at all," Noah said, smirking in Easton's direction.

Easton scratched at his nose. "I got worried. Okay?"

Lou found Easton's obvious worry for the horse endearing, but she chose not to point it out for fear of making him uncomfortable. Noah walked forward to join Willow in her inspection of OC. Willow had ducked between the fence posts and stepped into the paddock. She was running her hands up and down the horse's legs. Lou and Easton remained on the other side of the fence.

"It's just this one scrape," Willow said, checking with Noah. "It doesn't seem deep enough to need stitches, does it?"

Noah shook his head even before he knelt next to the cut to get a better view. Once he'd inspected it for a few seconds, he said, "Nope. Let's just clean it out and put ointment on it. If you repeat that at least once a day, he should be healed up in no time."

"Sorry to call Noah out for all that," Easton called to Willow. "I might've been overzealous with my worry."

Willow sent her neighbor a genuine smile—not a hint of

snark or sarcasm to be found. "No, it's great. I appreciate you taking the highest precautions around this guy. He's my entire world." Willow glanced over her shoulder. "Besides you, Lou." The goat bounded into the paddock at that moment as if he knew she'd forgotten him. "And you, too, Steve."

While Noah and Willow cleaned out OC's wound, Lou and Easton waited in the yard.

"So ..." Lou said, peering over at the detective, "any news about Credence's cause of death?" Sure, there had been the pill bottle at the scene, but that could've been a decoy, a misdirection placed there by the killer along with a suicide note.

Easton dipped his chin closer to his chest. Lou couldn't tell if it was a sort of nod or a gesture of fatigue. "Not yet. The ME's office is pretty backed up."

And it's not a top priority since they all think it's a suicide, Lou thought. She considered asking him about the time of death next, but Willow and Noah were finished with their bandaging and walked over. Willow told Noah he could head home if he needed to go, but he insisted on sticking around.

"Cass has Marigold tonight, so I'm free," he said, punctuating the sentence with the dimpled smile that appeared any time he talked about his daughter.

Lou couldn't help but think about what Willow had shared earlier about Noah and Cassidy's divorce. She felt for Noah, knowing the end to any relationship was never easy, but especially one that had lasted through so many formative years.

"Can I get anyone a drink?" Willow asked as they wandered over to her deck. "Water? Beer? Wine?"

"I'd take a beer," Noah said. "It's been quite the week." He pulled up a chair at the outdoor patio table Willow had just put the cushions on last week in the warm weather.

Easton held up a finger and nodded, signaling he'd like a beer as well. Then he slumped into the seat next to Noah.

"Sure. Water for me, please." Lou placed the high school yearbooks on the table, happy to be rid of their weight.

"Oh, wow. I haven't seen one of these for a while." Noah reached for the same one Easton had picked up before. He flipped it open and paged through for a moment before stopping on a spread about the baseball team. His eyes glowed with a reminiscent spark as he found himself in the team lineup. "Man, I thought I was a big deal back then." He shook his head.

A picture of him on the pitcher's mound sat centered on the page. Young Noah wore a confident smirk as he wound up to throw.

The group laughed, knowing they'd all had illusions of grandeur in their formative years.

"You were an okay pitcher. Nothing like Cass, though," Easton said with a teasing smile as he flipped to the fastpitch page.

The page featured a young Cassidy, her expression hard and focused.

"Both of you were pitchers on your high school teams?" Lou asked in surprise.

Noah nodded. "We played in college as well. You should see Marigold's arm. That girl can throw like no one's business. We signed her up for a rec league this year, and instead of keeping her with the other nine-year-olds, they moved her up to the twelve-year-old group because she was so good. Why do you have these?" Noah asked, glancing up at Willow and Lou.

"We're combing through old year books to get ideas for Spring Fling decorations," Lou explained.

"The person who's done it the last few years isn't being very helpful," Willow said as she came through the sliding glass door, balancing Lou's cup of water with two beers.

"Let me guess," Noah said, rolling his eyes.

"Mary." Easton let out a groan. He gestured for the yearbook closest to him and Noah handed it over. "I can't believe she was in my class," he mumbled as he flipped through the class pictures.

"Grumpy Mary is the same age as you?" Willow scoffed.

Lou shared in her friend's surprise. Mary looked and acted much older than thirty-eight. Maybe it was her irritable attitude.

Easton and Noah nodded.

"Here ..." Easton pointed to a picture of a teenage girl whose face was already soured into a sneer.

Lou's heart hurt at the thought that Mary had already been that jaded at such a young age.

"Having Mary in your class was a lot better than having Credence," Noah said, flipping forward to the senior class pictures. He stopped on a picture of a young Credence Crowley. "I know it's not right to speak ill of the dead, but that guy made our lives awful."

"Yeah, well, at least he was scared of you, Noah. He was even harder on the lower classmen," Easton told Lou and Willow. The same sourness evident in Mary's picture took over his countenance. "It's actually how Noah and I got to be friends. He stood up to Credence when he was giving me a hard time one day."

Memories seemed to hit Noah all at once. From the frown that twisted his mouth, they weren't good ones. "Too many of my friends came that way," he said.

"So Credence wasn't just a bully as an adult?" Willow asked.

"Nope. He's been practicing his whole life." Easton rubbed at his neck as if he could still feel the hands gripping the back of it. "On some of us more than others."

Discomfort grew inside Lou at Noah's change in tone, and now Easton's obvious hatred for the man. She'd had her fair share of bullies in junior high and high school, so she understood. Still, it surprised her to hear them talk like this about anyone. The two of them had been kind and warm to her ever since she'd moved to Button, and she didn't enjoy seeing these jaded versions of them.

"So ... Spring Fling. What should Willow know?" Lou asked, changing the subject to something more comfortable.

The guys took a moment to loosen up after the topic of

Credence, but within minutes, they were talking animatedly about the popular local festival.

"Marigold's looking forward to the cakewalk," Noah said, lacing his fingers behind his head. "You have all the cakes lined up?"

Willow chewed on her lip. "Yes, I think Johnny was just waiting to hear from his aunt about what she was going to make, but we have enough."

"I'd be happy to run the dunk booth," Easton offered. "I've done it before and it's really fun."

"Run it or volunteered to sit in the tank?" Willow cocked an eyebrow.

Easton shrugged. "Whatever you need me to do. Anything in the name of charity, right?" He laughed.

They stayed until the sun began to set and Willow had to feed the animals. Noah offered to drive Lou home, and she accepted the ride, not wanting Willow to have to drive her and knowing Noah would have to drive past her place anyway. But that night, instead of focusing on the warm laughter and fun she'd had with her friends, Lou couldn't help but ruminate about Credence.

The way the mere mention of him had changed two good men into scowling grumps made her wonder. Hate that strong would certainly take away any motivation for Easton to investigate into his former bully's death any more than he had to. The terrible thought sat in a pit at the bottom of Lou's stomach.

Because, the truth was, if she decided not to care about Credence's case, it was likely no one else would.

CHAPTER 7

L ou couldn't let go of the knowledge that Easton had been bullied by Credence back in high school. It consumed her thoughts the next morning as she got ready for the day. And as much as she empathized with the detective—she wasn't sure what she would do if she was in charge of the investigation into her high school bully's death—she felt compelled to dig a little more. Maybe if she had any downtime in the shop that day, she would.

She opened the shop and fell into the routine of the bookstore. She entered a stack of new books into the system, pet the cats, explained the adoption requirements and process to a few interested shoppers, rang up purchases, and helped customers search for books.

Silas settled into his normal spot with a newspaper. Forrest followed shortly after, but in an unusual turn of events, he held his coffee toward Lou.

"What's this?" she asked, taking it from him.

"The new guy made me the wrong drink." He tugged at the hem of his knit vest. "But Ruby said you sometimes order one of these. It's a lavender latte."

Lou's eyes widened. She loved having them as the occasional treat. "Oh, I do."

"It's yours, then." Forrest settled into his usual chair. "Ruby said she'd bring my correct order over in a few."

As if on cue, Ruby, the manager of the Bean and Button, entered the shop holding a to-go coffee cup. She was probably in her fifties—judging by the wrinkles around her eyes and the gray showing in her brown hair—but she was perkier than most people half her age. Lou wondered whether it was just her personality or whether working around coffee had something to do with her limitless supply of energy. Ruby's gaze settled on Forrest, and she smiled.

"Sorry about that, Forrest," she said. "I think he's having a hard time hearing customers when they order. This is the third one today." She fiddled with her green apron. "Though I'm not sure how your flat white became a lavender latte in his ears."

Forrest smiled. "No worries. Thanks for bringing it over."

Ruby sighed and looked around. "Man, maybe there's a reason the new kid can't hear. Compared to the noise of the coffee shop, this is a peaceful paradise. I think I need to come hang out around here more often." She swept her arms out, motioning toward all the cats lounging in the midmorning sunbeams.

"Did Liza end up contacting my lawyer friend?" Forrest asked Ruby.

"She did. Thanks. He says he has to look into Credence's will first, but he's optimistic." Ruby shrugged. "Okay, I'm back at it. Have a lovely day, everyone." She disappeared out the door and jogged back across the street to the coffeehouse.

Ruby's mention of Credence's will piqued Lou's interest, and she wandered over to where Forrest sat. "What was that all about?"

Forrest took a sip of his coffee. "Ruby's friends with Liza Osborne."

"Lou's too new to know about that whole scandal," Silas muttered from behind his newspaper.

"Right." Forrest slapped his palm onto his forehead. "I keep forgetting you just moved here. Gosh, where do I start with the story?"

Silas cleared his throat, proving he knew exactly where to start. "Liza Osborne is the adult daughter of a local couple who moved to town about twenty years ago. They're both passed now. For her father, that was just a few years after they moved here, but her mother just passed in January." He set his newspaper down. "Liza's been going through the house and her parents' possessions over the last few months, trying to figure out what to keep, what to sell, and clean up the house so she can put it on the market. But she didn't have a clue what to do with her father's old car that had been sitting in the garage since he passed in the late nineties."

"She thought it was a piece of junk, mostly because it looked like it." Forrest jumped in. "It was rusted; the paint was chipped, and it wouldn't run. Liza didn't want to spend the money to get it towed to Kirk, so she asked Credence to come give her an idea of what it was worth." Forrest rolled his eyes, and Lou could already tell this didn't end well.

"Credence told her it was a piece of junk and made her pay him five hundred to haul it away." Silas snorted.

"What he didn't tell Liza is that it was a sixty-seven Shelby Mustang. Collectors are always searching for those to refurbish, so all he had to do was get it running, and he had a buyer waiting to pay *over a hundred grand*." Forrest's words slowed at the end, to emphasize the price.

Lou's eyes went wide. "You're kidding."

Silas and Forrest shook their heads in tandem.

"He'd been trying to keep the potential sale quiet. Liza couldn't find the title and filed for a lost title, but it hadn't come in the mail yet. Credence hauled the car, saying Liza could just sign the title over to him whenever it showed up. All the while, he was taking bids from buyers online. He probably would've gotten away with it, too, but nothing ever stays a secret in this small town, and word got back to Liza. Ever since then, Liza's been looking into legal avenues to get the car back from him. The fact that it was just sitting in Credence's garage was driving her crazy," Forrest explained.

"Something that expensive is just sitting at his auto repair shop?" Lou asked.

"No," Silas said. "He moved it to his personal garage, but I'm not sure that's much safer."

Lou sipped at her lavender latte and pondered what she'd just learned. "That's intense."

But as she wandered back to the register counter to enter a new shipment of books, she realized that if she really was going to get serious about looking into Credence's death, Liza Osborne was a good place to start.

Lou lost herself in research about the Liza and Credence connection during a lull later that day. She started by searching for Liza Osborne on social media, hoping the woman had an account on one of the popular platforms that might hold information she could use. After a few minutes of browsing, Lou found her. The woman was blonde and appeared to be in her fifties, like Ruby. She had a wide smile and rosy cheeks.

She sure doesn't look like a murderer, Lou thought to herself as she searched through the woman's public profile.

But then Lou's attention caught on a lengthy post from a few months prior. Liza had included a picture of the car below the text.

Please help! This is my late father's Mustang. A man swindled me out of it, and I need to get it back. And before you jump to conclusions, it's not about the money. When I asked Credence Crowley to come look at the car, I did not know its emotional worth to my father. But shortly after Mr. Crowley convinced me it was a piece of junk, and something I should pay him to haul away, I found a photo album of my father with that car. Apparently, before I came along, that car was Dad's baby. According to the album I found, and the handwritten notes throughout from my mother, my dad washed that car weekly. He spent every weekend detailing the inside. When I came along, he put his time, energy, and money into me instead. It's part of why I never realized its value. Well, that and how he always called it his "bucket of bolts." I always thought that meant the car was worthless, but it turned out to be an endearing nickname. Based on the captions he wrote under some of the pictures, he'd been calling it that ever since he bought it. Once I was in his life, he treated that car just like any old vehicle. It fell into disrepair, especially once my dad passed away when I was in my thirties, and Mom didn't have the heart to even take it out of the garage. So, you see, the sentimental value this car holds for me is far greater than the sale Mr. Crowley hopes to make. I couldn't find the title when Mr. Crowley took the car, but a new one has been issued, which means I'm the legal title holder. If anyone knows of legal avenues I might take, I would appreciate the help.

So that was how Forrest knew to recommend a lawyer to Liza to help with her cause. Lou expected it would be fairly easy for her to get the car back now that she had a new title, but maybe it was more complicated than she realized.

As heartbreaking as the story was, the emotional value of the car rather than its monetary worth made Liza more of a suspect in Lou's eyes. Lou blinked, feeling the fatigue of staring at the computer screen for so long.

It was then that she realized it was past time to close the bookshop. She'd been so entrenched in Liza's car drama that she hadn't even noticed the time.

Racing over to the door to flip the closed sign and lock the door, Lou paused as she noticed her best friend pull up in a white truck with *Button School District — Official Use Only* stenciled onto the door.

Opening the door, Lou jogged outside. "Sorry, I totally forgot I was supposed to come help today. I got lost in some research."

Willow waved a hand but went around to the back of the truck and let down the tailgate. "No worries. I brought you some new friends." She flourished her hands toward four potted trees.

"You didn't have to do that." Lou placed a hand over her heart as she took in their lush green leaves.

"Actually, I did." Willow knelt down and hefted one pot toward the end of the tailgate where Lou could reach it. "These puppies aren't doing so well and need some direct morning light. I've seen the cats lounging in that morning sun on the weekends."

"The front of the building does get a lot of sun," Lou confirmed.

"Perfect. I was keeping these on the east side of the greenhouse, but the football team has decided they're fair game and keep ripping at their leaves as they jog by," Willow said through gritted teeth.

"I'd be happy to watch them." Lou picked up the first tree and tottered it over to the front window, noticing a few ripped and missing leaves as she set it in place.

She stepped back as Willow placed another one on the other side of the right front window. Inside the shop, the cats crowded around the window to see what the commotion was all about. Anne Mice stretched up, batting at the leaves through the glass. Once the other two were positioned on either side of the left window, Willow closed the tailgate.

"They're ash-leaf maples," Willow said. "They'll be pretty and leafy green throughout the spring and summer months."

"Thank you. How's Spring Fling planning going?" Lou asked through a grimace, still feeling bad she hadn't made it up to help today.

"It's fine. I've got the students working, and I feel pretty good about the decorations after our talk with the guys last night." Willow waved a hand at Lou. "What research were you doing?" she asked casually, obviously figuring it had to do with books.

Lou squinted one eye as she glanced over at the Bean and Button coffee shop. Through the front windows, she could see there were still a few customers inside. The coffee shop stayed open a little later than the bookstore, and Lou didn't want to chance talking about her suspicions about Liza within earshot of Ruby. She motioned for Willow to follow her inside.

Lou locked the door behind them. Willow stood there, expectation written all over her eager expression. "Well, this must be good if we had to come inside to talk about it."

"What do you know about Liza Osborne?" Lou asked, eyes darting over to watch a customer walk out of the coffee shop.

"Oh, you heard about the whole Mustang scandal, did you?" Willow asked, her eyes alight.

Lou nodded. "And I think she might've had cause to kill Credence."

Willow snorted. "Of course she did. The man cheated her out of over a hundred thousand dollars, but I'm guessing you read her whole emotional story about what the car meant to her dad. So you're trying to see if there's anything linking her to Credence's 'suicide'?"

"I think so, but it doesn't sound like she lives in town. Do you know when she's supposed to be here next?" Lou asked.

"No, but I know who will." Willow jerked a thumb toward the café across the street. "She and Ruby are friends."

Lou wrinkled her nose. "I know, I was hoping *not* to involve Ruby since she is such a good friend."

"Ruby doesn't have to know we suspect Liza of murder. We can just tell her we want to talk to Liza about something else," Willow suggested.

"Do you know what Liza does for a living?" Lou asked.

Willow squinted one eye. "I think she's a photographer, but don't quote me on that."

Low tapped her fingers against her leg as she fit that into their plan. "That's perfect. We can tell Ruby we're interested in talking to her about taking photographs for the Spring Fling festival."

"The photography club does that." Willow shook her head. When Lou gave her a pointed look, Willow added, "Oh, I see. Not for real. Gotcha."

Locking up the bookshop, they crossed the street and ordered two small lattes. Ruby must've been closing that day, because she was the only one left in the coffee shop.

When she handed over their lattes, Willow asked, "Hey, Ruby. Your friend Liza takes pictures, right?"

"She does," Ruby said. "Do you want her card? I have a few in my wallet." She gestured toward the back room of the café.

Lou held up both her hands. "That's not necessary. We can just touch base with her next time she's in town. Do you know when that's going to be?"

"She should be here this weekend." Ruby smiled. "She usually comes on Friday night unless she's had a long week in the city. If that's the case, she comes in on Saturday morning."

She visits on the weekends, Lou thought.

She didn't know exactly what day or time Credence had died, but she felt certain he'd been dead for at least a day when she'd found him on Monday. And Hannah had seen him in the grocery store buying cake and vodka on Thursday. That left Friday, Saturday, or Sunday—the weekend, which meant Liza would've had the opportunity to kill him if she was in town.

"Perfect, we'll catch her this weekend, then," Willow said, seeing Lou was deep in thought.

They turned and took their coffees back to the bookshop to make a plan for what they might say if they ran into Liza that weekend. Seeing as it was only Wednesday, it seemed like the weekend would take forever to get here, but Lou knew there was plenty to do in the meantime.

She may have discounted Timothy as a suspect, but in a town full of people who hated Credence, Liza couldn't be the only one who despised him enough to kill him.

CHAPTER 8

L ou had already been planning on helping Willow with Spring Fling preparations after work on Thursday, but an email she received about halfway through the day made her trip up to the high school even more of a priority.

It was from Evelyn Walters, the librarian. It said, *I wasn't sure when you were coming to work on those boxes of donated books, so I tried moving them out into the library for you. My knee hurt too much when I tried, so they're still back in the storeroom. Have to run the grandson to his driving class right after school today. Let yourself back there if you come while I'm out.*

Lou winced in sympathy, wishing Evelyn hadn't tried to move heavy boxes; Lou had promised she would go through them. She supposed that *had* been three days ago. Between Spring Fling planning with Willow and looking into Credence's death, she'd run out of time. Lou responded to Evelyn's email, letting her know she would be by that afternoon to take care of the books, hoping that would keep Evelyn from trying to do too much.

So even though it was Thursday, Lou closed a couple of hours early. She changed into her running gear and jogged up to the high school thinking maybe she could take a long route home to fit a run in after her work at the school was done.

She texted Willow before she left the bookstore.

> Heading to the high school. I have to get through those donated books in the library. Come see me if you have time!

Willow responded.

> I'll come find you once I extract myself from this dunk tank.

> Why are you putting together the dunk tank this early? The festival's not until next week, right?

> A kid mentioned that one year they didn't check it early, and it had a huge leak in the side. Ruined that whole booth.

She added a cringing emoji.

> Not on my watch.

Lou laughed at her friend and gave her message a thumbs-up.

At the high school, Lou went straight to the library. The lights were off, proving Lou must've just missed Evelyn. Lou stepped inside, smiling at the sweet, musty smell of books. That smile fell away as she flipped on the lights and was met with the messy stacks of books cluttering the space, yet another red flag that the poor librarian was overwhelmed. Lou wondered how much of an imposition it would be to shelve some of them for Evelyn.

She pressed her lips together and decided to tackle the boxes of books in the back first. She was just plucking a yellow legal pad and a pen from the circulation desk to write the titles when the library door swung open, and Evelyn rushed inside, limping on her bad knee.

"Oh, you're back." Lou smiled, but it quickly dropped into a frown as she noticed Evelyn's worried expression. "Is everything okay?"

The woman bustled past her. She let out a loud exhale. "Yes, it is now." Evelyn pulled a purse out from behind the circulation desk. "Got one to his driving class and now another needs to go to soccer. Can you believe I left here without my purse? Goodness."

Lou actually *could* believe it with how busy Evelyn's schedule sounded.

Evelyn must've sensed Lou's pity, because she waved a hand at her and said, "It won't be like this for long. My eldest grandson turns sixteen next month, so he'll be able to help with some of the driving. Agreeing to drive around his siblings is one of the few reasons he got that ridiculous car he wanted so badly." She rolled her eyes.

"Ridiculous?" Lou asked.

"Oh," Evelyn said with a huff. "It's this bright purple monstrosity with a huge wing bolted to the back. He loves it, and it was the right price." She clicked her tongue once.

Wait. Lou had seen a car like that on her runs through town. It took her a moment to place where she'd noticed it. "Do you live out on Needle Street, across from Credence Crowley?" Lou asked, excitement quickening her words.

Evelyn lifted her chin. "I do. Are you out that way too?" she asked, checking her watch.

"No, but I was at Mr. Crowley's home trying to deliver a book to him the other day. I was the one who found his body," she said, the steam behind her sentence dissipating quickly.

Lou waited for Evelyn to say something grouchy about Credence, like everyone else in the town had a tendency to do when they heard his name. But the woman's face softened.

"Ah, such a terrible story." She stared at the wall for a moment.

"You knew him well?" Lou asked, intrigued by the only person in town who didn't seem to hate Credence.

Evelyn tsked. "No one really did. Kept to himself mostly."

"You didn't see anything odd around his house that weekend, did you?" Lou asked, hating to disrupt the memories Evelyn seemed to be recalling in that moment.

Evelyn narrowed her eyes as she thought. "You know, now that you mention it, there was a woman sneaking around the place when I took the trash out on Friday night, around seven."

"Woman?" Lou's interest piqued.

"Blonde. Trying to hide in a black turtleneck, but really just making herself stand out." Evelyn wrinkled her nose with distaste.

Blonde? Like Liza Osborne.

Evelyn continued to rant. "You know, if Credence wanted to have women companions over, he didn't need to have them sneak around. He was a grown man."

"Do you think it's possible that she wasn't there to see Credence for a good reason?" Lou tiptoed around the words, not wanting to be offensive.

"What do you mean?" Evelyn asked gently, checking her watch one more time.

Lou didn't want to make Evelyn late for her next drop off, so she said, "Nothing. Never mind. I'll go work on going through those donated books in the back."

Evelyn waved. "Perfect. You can't miss them. They're stacked right inside." She pointed to a door at the back of the library.

Once Evelyn left, Lou contemplated the clue the librarian had just given her about a mysterious woman sneaking around Credence's house on Friday night.

She pushed through the door and into the storage room. Three large boxes sat in between metal shelving units that held everything from cardboard boxes to seasonal decorations for the library.

There was a note taped to the flaps on the top box.

Enjoyed losing myself in the books from this library so much during my years at Button High; I thought I would add to the collection.
- Carol Joyce

A lightness radiated through Lou. She had also found her high school library to be a place of solace. Pulling open the first box, Lou got started on her list.

The first box took her a half hour to go through and document. Carol had good taste, and there were quite a few classics in that bunch. She was pulling the last few books out from the second box, which seemed to be mostly epic fantasy novels, when Willow stumbled inside.

"Holy smokes, it's a dust pit back here." She waved a hand in front of her face.

Lou had sneezed approximately twenty-nine times since she sat down, so she was well aware.

"Yeah." Lou sneezed again. "Tell me about it." She squinted up at her friend. "Hey, so Evelyn said she saw a strange blonde woman sneaking around Credence's place on Friday night. She's convinced it was some sort of lady friend of Credence's, but I think it could've been the person who hurt him, and I think that person might be Liza Osborne." Lou moved the empty cardboard box aside so she could open the third and last box.

"Could be," Willow said. "Especially since she's your only suspect right now."

Lou stood and dusted off her running pants before opening the final box. The tape peeled right off, and she flipped back the cardboard flaps.

"Oh, look," she said as she recognized what sat on top of this collection of books.

"What?" Willow asked, craning her neck to see inside.

Lou picked up the large volume and showed Willow. "It's a Button High yearbook. One year before the one we were flipping through with Noah and Easton at your house."

Willow made a grabbing gesture at the book. "Oh, that means we're going to get a peek at sophomore Easton. I wonder if he looks even goofier." She giggled as she flipped through the pages.

Easton looked fairly similar, but Willow still broke out into a fit of laughter as she pointed at his picture. Not finding it nearly as entertaining as Willow, Lou flipped forward into the junior class pages to search for Noah.

But before she could get to the Rs, Lou stopped on a page with C and D last names. It was hard to go past it, in fact.

Along the right side of the page, one picture was scratched out with black permanent marker as if the person had used angry, frantic strokes. Willow's laughter came to an abrupt halt as she pointed to the page. The name underneath the picture was Credence Crowley. Along the side of his picture was the chilling text, *Most likely to be murdered before he turns thirty-eight.*

Lou gulped. Willow exhaled.

"Credence would've been thirty-eight on Saturday," Lou said, remembering her discussion with the regulars in the bookshop the day before she found the body. "Which supports my conjecture that he died Friday night." Lou's voice sounded odd as it reverberated in the small, dusty space.

"I thought Friday night made us think it was Liza," Willow said.

Lou shrugged. "Maybe this Carol Joyce"—Lou read the name off the donation note—"is blonde too. She obviously hated Credence."

They paged through the yearbook and found a picture of Carol Joyce in the senior class list.

"She's got brown hair here, but that doesn't mean she hasn't dyed it since high school," Willow pointed out.

Young Carol wore thick glasses and had braces. Had Credence bullied her until she cracked?

"I don't think Liza is our only suspect anymore," Lou whispered. "By the looks of this, Carol Joyce hated Credence enough to write about killing him."

CHAPTER 9

Closing Carol Joyce's yearbook, Lou cradled it under her arm. She surveyed the mess of books. "I'm going to have to finish this tomorrow. We need to find Carol. Do you know where she works? Or if she even still lives in town?"

"She might not," Willow said. "I've never heard of her. Maybe the ladies in the office will know. They usually know everything."

They made their way down to the office, and Lou tucked the list of books from the donation box inside the yearbook. The office smelled like stale coffee and spring flowers. The stale coffee was probably sitting in a coffeemaker in the back room, but the fresh flowers lit up Lou's vision right away. The registrar, Mrs. Kyle, had an enormous arrangement of blooms sitting on the desk in front of her, almost to the point that she couldn't see over them.

When she noticed Willow, she clasped her hands together. "Still enjoying my beauties," the registrar said, gesturing to the arrangement.

"I'm so glad." Willow beamed. To Lou, she said, "It's office administration appreciation month. We're showering them with gifts each week. The kids made them cards last week. It was so sweet."

Lou smiled, noticing that each of the office ladies had a beautiful arrangement of flowers at her desk. She knew she was biased but thought Willow must be their favorite teacher.

From the bags being packed and computers shutting down, the office staff must've been on their way out for the day. Lou realized they'd just caught them in time.

"You ladies wouldn't know anything about Carol Joyce, would you?" Willow asked, then added, "She used to be a student here. Is she still in town?"

"Yeah, she's still around. She's a nurse at the hospital," Mrs. Kyle said.

"Oh, perfect," Willow said. When she noticed Mary scowling at her, she added, "Lou just has some questions about the books she donated. Thanks!"

With that, they made their way out to the parking lot and climbed into Willow's car.

"To the hospital, it is." Willow started her car.

"Do you think we should ask Easton?" Lou wondered aloud.

Willow shook her head. "If he didn't believe you before, this isn't going to change his mind. Plus, we're not going to confront Carol about anything. We're just asking her a few questions about her yearbook. Once we see how she reacts to those, we can call Easton."

"Right," Lou said, paging through the yearbook.

Her stomach dropped as she came to a page in the last third that held jagged handwriting. She hadn't noticed it before.

Ugly Button, It's been nice knowing you. It's tragic that you'll kill yourself, alone in your house, before you're thirty-eight. - CC

Reading it aloud to Willow made Lou cringe. "What do you want to bet CC stands for Credence Crowley?"

Willow parked and shot Lou a worried glance. "So he made fun of Carol so much and told her she was going to kill herself before she turned thirty-eight, and it just happens to be how he died?" Willow clicked her tongue, like she often did when she was trying to get OC's attention. "Too coincidental, in my mind."

Lou left the yearbook in the car, and they walked inside.

The hospital was tiny compared to anything Lou had experienced in New York City, but it looked well equipped to handle anything the locals would need. They opted to enter through the regular entrance instead of the urgent care one, walking into a quiet waiting room that smelled like hydrogen-peroxide-soaked gauze. There were cream-colored chairs in a cream-colored waiting room, and Lou had to let her eyes adjust for a moment before she could see through all the similar tones, almost like letting them acclimate to the dark.

A handful of people sat in the waiting room filled with the usual soundtrack: coughing, a baby crying, phones ringing, and the beep of machines down the hall. Willow approached the man sitting at the reception desk.

"Hello." He met them with a smile.

"Hi," Willow said. "We're looking for Carol Joyce. Do you know if she's working today?"

The man's face lit up in recognition. His eyes flicked down to something next to his computer screen that Lou guessed was a schedule. "She's not here right now, but her shift starts in a few minutes. If you want to have a seat, I can call you over when she gets here."

Lou and Willow thanked him and took a seat.

"I thought we were out of luck," Willow whispered.

"Me too." Lou checked her watch. "If she starts her shift this late, that means she's working the night shift. I wonder how long that's been the case."

"Because if she was working Friday night, she couldn't have been the blonde woman Evelyn saw sneaking around Credence's house," Willow said, proving she was following Lou's logic.

"Unless she had that Friday night off." Lou scuffed the sole of her shoe against the cream-colored carpet.

"So what exactly are we going to ask her about the yearbook?" Willow asked.

Lou shrugged. "I figured we'd just be honest. We found it in the donation box and wanted to make sure it wasn't put in there by accident."

Willow laughed. "Right. That makes sense. The truth. I'm not sure why I didn't think of that." She shook her head.

A few minutes later, the man at the reception desk called them over. He waved to the woman behind him and said, "These women wanted to talk to you, Carol."

Carol appeared to be about their same age, which made sense since they knew when she'd graduated. But instead of having brown hair, like she used to in high school, now she had blonde hair, and her braces must've worked, because when she smiled, she revealed very straight, white teeth. She kept her grin broad even though she was obviously confused at not recognizing either Willow or Lou.

Lou's whole body tingled with anticipation. Carol was blonde.

"Hi. How can I help you?" she asked, motioning for them to follow her to the side of the long reception desk so they were out of the way as a couple stepped forward to check in for an appointment.

"I'm Willow, a teacher up at the high school." Willow placed a hand on her chest.

"And I'm Lou. I own the bookstore in town," Lou said.

"Oh, the one with the cats?" Carol's voice grew all high pitched like she'd just seen something cute. "I've been thinking about coming by, but I'm just not sure if my two would accept a new sister or brother."

"Totally understandable," Lou said. "I'm also helping order some new books for the high school library. Mrs. Walters said I should go through your donation box first to make sure I don't order any duplicates."

Carol's smile fell. "Is there something wrong with them?"

"Not at all," Lou said. "You brought in some great titles. It's just … we found your high school yearbook in one box, and we're afraid it made its way in there by accident." Lou held her breath as she waited for Carol's response.

Carol waved a hand at them. "Oh, that? No. That wasn't mine. That's sweet of you to check, though. I actually found it at the local charity shop one day a few years ago. It must've been inside a donation box. I figured it should be back at the high school instead of sitting there, so I added it to the stack."

Lou's shoulders dropped from their tensed state. "Oh. And you don't know whose it is?"

"No," Carol said. "I checked in the front cover where we used to write our names and I didn't see anything. There weren't any signatures in the front or back, either, so I thought it would be a good one to send back to the high school. I know they like to keep old copies."

Eyes narrowing as she listened to Carol talk, Lou realized she was either lying or hadn't checked the pages very well.

"So Credence Crowley didn't bully you in high school?" Willow asked, a little boldly, in Lou's opinion.

Carol must've been caught off guard by the question because she blinked a few times before answering. "Actually, I … no." She pressed her lips into a thin line for a moment. "I was one of the few he didn't since I had very big older brothers." Her mouth tipped up into a half smile. "I was lucky."

Lou frowned. "Would you mind telling us the names of the students who weren't so lucky? Were there any people who he paid extra attention to?" Lou grimaced as she said it, but she knew from experience that bullies often had specific targets they went after, repeatedly.

Carol winced but nodded. "From what I can remember, it was mostly Flora and Owen."

"Flora Henning?" Willow blurted out. "Principal Henning?"

Lou understood at the second question. Willow's boss.

"Well, she was Flora Lucas back then, but yeah. He always messed with her. And Owen Sanchez. That poor guy even got shoved in his locker once. It was a Friday after school, and no one found him for about five hours until his parents got concerned when he never came home from the chess club." Carol checked her watch. "I'm so sorry, but I'd better start my shift."

"Right," Lou said. "Thank you so much for taking the time to talk with us. And thank you for the book donation. It really is lovely."

Carol waved goodbye and turned to disappear through a galley-style door into the back hallway.

Lou and Willow wandered out to the car, the excitement gone from their steps.

"So it's likely not Carol," Willow said, her tone flat. "Not that I wanted it to be. She was really nice."

Lou agreed. "She could be lying, but she didn't tense up when we said Credence's name like the rest of his targets have. What about your boss? Does she have blonde hair?"

Willow snorted. "No. It's brown. And that lady is probably the least likely to hold a grudge, I've ever met. She seems super happy, and she's really outgoing. If she was bullied in high school, she didn't hold on to it."

Lou didn't push the issue, but she could not dismiss the idea of Flora as a suspect as quickly as Willow had. She knew Willow really respected her principal and had only good things to say about her, but Lou wasn't so sure that meant Flora was over what Credence had done to her.

Willow hadn't ever been the victim of bullying in school. She'd been too tall and too vocal for anyone to pick on, unlike shy, quiet Lou. It hadn't hurt that Willow had been on the lacrosse team for most of high school and carried her lacrosse stick around with her most places. And even though Willow stood up for Lou, she couldn't be by her side all the time. But Lou didn't want to get sucked into negative thoughts about things that had happened to her decades ago. They had a real problem to solve now.

"And Owen is a man, but he could have long hair. In the dark, Evelyn might have mistaken him for a woman sneaking around Credence's house on Friday night." Lou opened the passenger side door and got inside.

"That means, until we find out what Owen's hair looks like, we're still searching for this Liza gal. We'll have to wait until this weekend when she's in town again." Willow sighed as she buckled herself in.

Lou agreed that Liza was still a suspect, but now that they'd found this yearbook, it seemed more likely that someone from Credence's past could've killed him. She needed to find out his time of death, for sure, because if he'd died on the eve of his thirty-eighth birthday, it was too much of a coincidence. And if that was the case, the killer must've been planning Credence's murder for decades.

CHAPTER 10

"Okay, repeat the plan back to me." Lou paced in the bookshop Saturday morning. She stepped over cats as she walked, turning back toward Willow.

"I go across the street to Bean and Button. I wait inside and drink coffee while I finish entering my grades that aren't technically due until next week." Willow bounced her shoulders happily. "Sorry, I've just never been early getting my report cards done before." She shook her head and focused on Lou. "I will watch for Liza. If I see her, I'll text you."

Lou nodded along. "When I get your text, I'll put up this sign." She stopped and held up a printed sign saying she'd be back in a few minutes. "And I'll come join you in the coffeehouse."

"We're going to get her talking by mentioning that you're new in town and you're in the market for a car and that you heard she might have something to sell. You like older cars." Willow circled her hands as if she could see it all playing out in front of her.

"All of which is true," Lou said. "When she expresses frustration about what happened with the car, we'll side with her and talk about how awful Credence was to trick her like that."

"And then we'll say, 'Good thing he's gone.' Right?" Willow cringed, any excitement gone at the phrase. "Even though he was awful, it still feels like a terrible thing to say."

Lou shared in her friend's grimace. "I know, and if we heard about the car through the town grapevine, why wouldn't we have heard the news that Credence had taken it? It doesn't make sense. Maybe we go back to the idea of telling her she looks just like someone we saw across the street at Credence's house last Friday night."

"Pretend we live at Evelyn's house?" Willow wrinkled her nose. "This would be so much easier if we were Easton and could just walk up to people and say things like, 'Where were you on Friday between the hours of seven and ten?'"

Lou agreed. She pressed her fingertips into her temples as she tried to think.

"Actually…" Willow's voice curled conspiratorially.

"No." Lou bit out the word, knowing what her friend was considering. "Impersonating a police officer is a crime."

Willow's shoulders dropped. "How else could we find out what she was doing last Friday evening?"

"I think pretending to live at Evelyn's is the only way." Lou frowned.

Willow pressed her palms together as she thought. "Okay," she said. "You're right. It's our best shot. Let's hope it works." With that, she grabbed her bag and waved at Lou as she jogged across the street.

Even though Lou knew Willow was over there watching, she couldn't help but glance over each time she noticed someone entering or exiting Bean and Button.

"Whatcha lookin' at over there?" Silas asked an hour later. Both Catnip Everdeen and Jules Purrne sat next to him on the love seat.

Lou turned toward him. "Oh, nothing. Just noticing that there are a surprising number of people with blonde hair walking into the coffee shop today." Her eyes flicked back across the street and then back at Silas. "Do you ever notice stuff like that?" she asked him when his scowl only deepened.

"No," was his answer.

Lou pressed her lips together, but after only a moment, her gaze wandered back to the coffee shop. Another blonde woman walked up and opened the door. From across the street, Lou couldn't get a good enough look at any of her to tell if she was Liza. That would be up to Willow. Lou tensed, monitoring her phone for a notification from Willow. That was the third blonde woman this hour.

If it was Liza, this would be perfect timing. With Silas in the shop, she could just ask him to watch it for her for a few minutes and wouldn't even need to use the sign she'd made.

But neither that blonde, nor the next two, appeared to be Liza because another hour went by without a text from Willow. Silas left and grumbled something about her acting weird and how she was giving him the 'heebie-jeebies.'

It wasn't until almost noon when Lou got a message from Willow.

She's here!

Lou jumped, but just as she was grabbing her sign to lock up, a customer entered. It was a young man who wandered through each aisle at a snail's pace.

Normally, Lou loved it when people took their time in her store. As a book lover herself, she understood the necessity of making a first pass, then doing a closer examination of anything that caught her attention, and really feeling the need to get to know the book before she purchased it.

But right now, Lou needed to get across the street.

The man stopped to pet Puurt Vonnegut as he knelt to see the books on the lower shelves of the fantasy section.

She frantically typed out a message to Willow before addressing the young man.

Stall!

"Can I help you find something specific, or are you just browsing?" Lou asked in as airy of a tone as she could muster.

He tipped his head to one side. "Kind of. I'm looking for *Mistborn* by Brandon Sanderson."

"Sure. I have that." Lou typed the title into the computer just to make sure. "We have a used copy or a new one on the bottom shelf just in front of you."

"Oh, used would be great." The guy wandered over to the used section and ambled through as if he might search every shelf.

Lou popped over to its exact location and plucked it off the shelf. "Here you go." She smiled, handing it over to him.

"Thanks." His eyes wandered around the rest of the shop.

"Is that all? Or..." She considered saying something about him looking more, but she didn't want him to get any ideas. "Or would you like me to ring it up for you?"

The customer sent a longing gaze over his shoulder, but said, "Sure. Thanks."

Lou led him over to the register. Every part of her screamed in defiance. Rushing a person in a bookstore was a cardinal sin in her and Ben's eyes. She just had to believe that she was doing it for a good cause. If she learned something from Liza that could prove she was the one hanging around Credence's house on Friday night, then she could convince Easton to look into the case as something other than a suicide. Putting a calculating murderer behind bars had to be a worthy enough cause.

Lou handed over the customer's receipt and the book. She waited three seconds longer than she strictly felt comfortable with —another customer could've slipped inside at any moment—

before slapping the sign on the front door, locking it behind her, and jogging across the street.

She burst into the coffee shop with such force that everyone inside looked over in surprise. She waved awkwardly at the locals and then located Willow. But as she made her way over to her friend's table, she scanned the café.

She didn't see Liza anywhere.

"I missed her, didn't I?" Lou grumbled, slipping into the seat next to Willow.

"Nope." Willow pointed to a table with a to-go cup sitting alone. "She's in the bathroom. You're fine."

Lou glared at her friend. "You couldn't text me that? I practically burst a blood vessel in my eye willing a customer to find a book faster."

Willow's eyes twinkled. "It was kind of fun to watch you race over here."

Lou crossed her arms. "You're lucky I can't live without you."

Before they could argue anymore about Willow's communication skills, a blonde woman came back to a table from the back hallway where the bathrooms were located.

Lou and Willow held each other's gaze and nodded seriously, confirming that they both remembered the plan. They stood, walking over to Liza's table and slipping into empty seats next to and across from her.

"I'm sorry," Willow said. "This is going to sound a little weird, but—" Willow cut off as if her throat had suddenly gone dry.

Lou immediately understood why. Easton had just walked into the coffee shop.

"Uh…" Willow froze there, openmouthed, as Easton walked up to their table. He was dressed in a suit, but his detective's badge was visible on the chain he wore around his neck.

"Hey, what are you two up to?" He regarded Lou and Willow suspiciously. When they didn't answer, he looked at Liza, who shrugged.

"We were just..." Willow swallowed heavily like she was trying to keep the words from coming out.

Because they couldn't pretend they lived in Evelyn's house now that Easton was standing there. While Liza didn't live in town and wouldn't know they were lying, Easton sure would. They also couldn't tell him to mind his own business because that would just clue him in to the fact they were up to something.

Lou saw the urge telling him to get lost flit across Willow's face before she came to the same conclusion about it being a bad idea.

"We were just asking people some questions for a poll," Lou started, the words coming out warily as she thought of a new plan. "One of Willow's high school students is doing a statistics project and needs to ask as many people as possible to get his data."

Willow grinned, obviously liking the idea. "Yeah."

Liza sat forward, interested if not a little confused, as she waited for the question.

Easton crossed his arms. "Which student?" he asked suspiciously.

"Caden Kingsbury," Willow said, slowly at first and then the last name faster. "You know that little mathematic mind of his, always thinking up new projects."

"So you teach math now?" Easton asked.

"He's in my homeroom," Willow said. "They're *all our students* at Button High." She lifted her chin proudly, repeating something she must've heard at a motivational teacher training. "Just trying to help in any way I can. He didn't go for my idea to poll people on their favorite type of house plant." She laughed.

Easton didn't. He sat in the last vacant seat at the table. "What's the question."

Lou pressed her lips together. "What were you doing last Friday night? Wasn't that it, Willow?"

Willow kept a straight face. "Yep, that was the wording."

Liza's frown had deepened, and her smile dropped. "Well, it looks like you have someone to ask, so I'm going to—" She moved to leave.

But Willow's hand shot out and landed on Liza's arm, stopping her. "No, please stay. We need as many people to answer the question as possible." Willow locked her eyes on Liza and repeated the question. "What were you doing last Friday night?"

"Like yesterday?" Easton interrupted.

Lou and Willow shook their heads simultaneously. Liza gulped.

"No. Last Friday," Willow said.

"He didn't even tell Willow about the project until yesterday, so last night wouldn't have happened yet. He wants his data to be consistent," Lou said, squaring her shoulders. She repeated, "Last Friday, between seven and ten on Friday night." She studied Easton's reaction for clues about whether she was right about the time window.

His expression remained unreadable.

"Oh, that's easy," Liza said with a smile. "I was at a movie. I saw a movie. Here in town," she added, then she moved to stand.

This time Easton held out a hand to stop her. His focus swiveled around the table. "Hold on, Liza. I'm sorry. I'm guessing the student is going to want to know which movie it was. Am I correct?"

Willow nodded, but Lou tapped her foot under the table as she worked through the implications of Liza's alibi. A movie. That meant she wasn't their blonde lurker.

Liza bit her lip. "It was … I think … ha ha, I can't believe I forgot already. Let me see…" She scrunched up her nose, but her eyes darted around the room nervously.

Easton's stare moved from Lou and Willow to Liza. Lou keyed in on the suspicious behavior as well. Easton opened his mouth to say something.

But before he could, Liza blurted out, "Okay, you caught me. I was sneaking around Credence's house Friday night."

Easton coughed while Lou and Willow sat back in surprise.

Liza shook her head even though no one had asked her a question. "I didn't do anything. I swear. I found my dad's spare key for the Mustang, and I thought maybe I could go steal it back from Credence since he basically stole it from me. But I chickened out when I got to the whole breaking into his garage part. I couldn't go through with it."

Her face was red, and her eyes watered like the pressure of tears was building up and she might burst into sobs at any moment.

Easton, a professional, calmly said, "Liza, I'm sorry. We—I wasn't trying to trap you into saying anything like that. You don't have to be upset."

Tears began spilling down her cheeks. "I'm sorry. It wasn't like me. I was just so angry, and I figured it was only fair since I hold the title." She sniffed.

Lou felt an odd sense of relief, but Willow still wasn't convinced.

"And you didn't go inside his house at all?" Willow asked with narrowed eyes.

Liza blew her nose. "No. I swear."

But even with Easton there, Lou couldn't miss the opportunity. "Liza, while you were sneaking around, did you notice anything odd about Credence's house? Did you see anyone else in there with him?"

Liza swiped the back of her hand under her nose. "No one else was there that I could see." She ran her fingers along the top of her to-go cup thoughtfully. "But it looked like someone had been."

"Why?" Easton asked this time.

"There was a package on his doorstep," Liza said.

"What kind?" Lou asked.

Liza sniffed. "From the porch light, all I could see was a plate with blue cellophane wrapped around it. There was a metallic bow on top. But I didn't stick around for very long."

A plate of something with blue cellophane and a bow. Like someone had dropped off a birthday meal? Or baked goods?

"I'd better get going," Liza said, gesturing to her to-go cup of coffee.

Lou opened her mouth to say something that might stop the woman—she still had more questions—but Easton shot her a glare that told her she was out of line. Once they were alone, Easton pinched at the bridge of his nose, squeezing his eyes shut tight.

"Easton, I didn't see any blue cellophane or a bow in Credence's kitchen the day I was there." Lou leaned forward.

Keeping his eyes closed, Easton said, "I did. It was in his garbage can."

"So he ate whatever was on the plate," Lou mused.

"What are you two up to?" Easton asked, finally opening his eyes.

"Nothing," Willow said innocently. "Since when is it a crime to help one of my students with a school project?"

Lou had to give it to Willow. It showed commitment to stick with the completely fabricated story even when Easton so obviously knew they were lying.

He pointed at Willow and then Lou. "You two need to drop whatever it is you think you're doing."

Willow put her hands up in surrender. "Fine. We won't bug Liza anymore," she said as Easton got up and went to the counter to order his coffee. Under her breath, and only to Lou, Willow added, "Because now that we know it wasn't her, we're going to be too busy looking into the people Credence bullied in high school."

89

CHAPTER 11

The sounds and smells of the coffee shop pulsed around Lou. Thoughts and theories crowded inside Lou's mind, making her feel slightly claustrophobic for a moment. It didn't help that five new customers entered after Liza left. They all got in line behind Easton, who stepped forward to order his coffee.

The boost in business made Lou realize she needed to get back to the bookshop. But before she left, she had to take care of something.

Lou agreed with Willow. If Liza really had been sneaking around Credence's house to steal back her father's car, that meant Owen and Flora were their new focus. And something about it felt right. It made sense for Credence's death to have been planned over a long period of time, after decades of injustices.

The plate of baked goods left on Credence's doormat gave Lou pause as well. Was there actually someone who liked the man enough to leave him something for his birthday, or was it a clue that might point her toward the killer's identity?

One thing about their conversation with Liza was clear: if they wanted to get any information out of these suspects, they were going to need Easton's help. Willow might be willing to go on with the investigation behind his back, but Lou felt strongly that the local detective needed to know all the facts.

"We need to show Easton the yearbook," Lou whispered to Willow, nodding toward where he stood, waiting for his coffee.

Willow groaned. "But why?"

"If we want to investigate Credence's old targets, they're much more likely to tell the truth with a detective," Lou said. "You saw how Liza lied at first, but Easton's presence at the table made her blurt out the truth."

Willow puffed out her cheeks and exhaled. "I guess you're right."

She didn't protest as Lou called Easton back over to the table once he'd received his coffee.

"What's up?" he asked, sipping warily.

Lou stood. "Can you follow us back to the bookshop? I have to open up again, but we have something to talk to you about."

Easton glanced at Willow, who rolled her eyes—still mad he needed to be involved—but he reluctantly nodded.

"Okay," he said. "I guess I have a few minutes." He followed them across the street to the bookshop.

The sun shone, and birds sang in the trees as they reached the other side of the sidewalk. Lou almost wished she could prop the front door open. The breeze felt so nice, but the cats would surely get out. She thought about how much it might cost to install a screen door for the summer months.

Lou took down the printed sign and unlocked the door. Then she turned to face the detective. "I know you think Credence killed himself, but there are things that just don't add up, Easton. And maybe nothing will come of it, and I'll have to admit I was wrong, but wouldn't you rather be sure?"

Easton looked up at the ceiling for a moment, but he brought his attention back to Lou. "How'd you figure out the time of death? Did someone at the station tell you two?" he asked, sitting on the love seat next to Jules Purrne.

"Because his birthday was Saturday," Willow said as if it were all the proof he needed.

When Easton stared at her, eyebrows arched in question, Lou brought over the yearbook she'd been keeping behind the bookstore's checkout counter. She handed it over to him.

"Willow and I found this old yearbook in a box of donated books from Carol Joyce," she explained, pointing out the hateful note someone with the initials C.C. had left near the back. "Credence was the only person who signed it. He addressed it to 'Ugly Button.' Does that nickname sound familiar to you?" Lou asked Easton, knowing he'd been a year younger than Credence and might've heard him calling someone that name.

Easton's posture tensed, but he shook his head. "The only names I heard Credence call people were much worse than that."

Lou continued on with the explanation. "It can't be a coincidence that he wrote this terrible thing about a person killing themselves before they turned thirty-eight, and then this shows up in the same yearbook." Lou directed him to the picture of Credence that had been crossed out, along with the *Most likely to be murdered before he turns thirty-eight* threat.

Scratching between his eyebrows, Easton said, "Well, I was going to fault you for jumping to the conclusion that C.C. stood for Credence, but this makes it pretty clear."

"We think the killer might be one of his old bully victims, and that they've been planning this for twenty years all because of what he wrote in their yearbook," Willow said.

Easton closed the yearbook. "The medical examiner already ruled Credence's death a suicide. He died of an overdose of sleeping pills. He wrote a note. Everything is consistent."

"Were the sleeping pills the only thing in his stomach?" Lou asked, thinking about what they'd just learned from Liza about the plate of baked goods.

"Just a couple of peanut butter cookies," Easton said, his tone made it clear how unimportant he found the information.

Lou leaned forward. "He didn't touch the cake he bought, and you said the plate was in the trash. Cookies could've been what was on the plate Liza saw on his porch."

"The person could've drugged him through the cookies," Willow said, showing she was on the same page as Lou.

But Easton wasn't. "There had to be close to thirty sleeping pills in Credence's stomach. There's no way someone hid that many inside a few cookies. The autopsy showed that was the only poison. From the bottle he left on the counter, it had to be over twenty since he'd filled it recently. I'm sorry to tell you, but he did this on purpose."

Lou's shoulders dropped, showing her disappointment. "You don't think someone might've baked sleeping pills into the cookies left on his porch?"

"That's not really a thing. Baking the cookies would compromise the active ingredients in the sleeping pills. And I think Credence would notice if someone shoved a sleeping pill into the middle of an already baked cookie," he scoffed.

Biting her lip as she thought, Lou said, "What if they only put a couple in the cookies? Enough to get him drowsy so they could sneak inside and..." Lou's explanation petered out.

"And shoved the rest of the pills down his throat," Willow said, picking up the thought.

Easton inhaled, but Lou could see the idea had gotten him thinking.

"If you have even a sliver of doubt that this could've been a murder, you have to listen to us, Easton," Lou begged.

He exhaled the breath he'd been holding on to. "Fine. Convince me by telling me who you suspect." He pulled out his notepad.

Willow and Lou shared a triumphant smile before joining him in the seating area.

"Okay, so at first we were thinking it was Timothy Davis, because he was so mad at Credence for the car troubles he had on his way to the reunion." Lou curled her fingers into fists in her lap as she spoke, willing Easton to be open-minded as he listened.

To his credit, the detective said, "A valid motive, not to mention the way he's been driving menacingly past Credence's house ever since he got back. I could see it. Next?" Easton asked, his patience still intact.

Lou turned toward Willow. "Next would be Liza. Evelyn Walters is Credence's neighbor. She said she saw a blonde woman sneaking around Credence's house on Friday night. That's how we knew to question Liza. But I'm not sure we can trust what she just told us. I would dig into that alibi a little more. She definitely hated the guy, had cause to want him dead, and was on his property the night he was murdered."

The cats paced through the bookshop, sensing the intense energy of the conversation happening between the people. Even Jules picked up her head and moved to another side of the shop, annoyed that they'd invaded her slumbering spot to have their discussion. Lou reached down and scooped up Anne Mice as she passed by, petting her but keeping an eye on the detective.

Easton finished writing. "Next?"

"Carol Joyce is another suspect. She was the one who donated the yearbook to the high school. She must not have looked inside, because she said she found it in the local charity shop like it had been in a donation box," Willow explained. "She could've been lying, though."

"She usually works nights, but it's possible she had last Friday off." Lou scrunched her fingers into the gray cat's soft fur as she talked.

"Carol also told us Credence's primary targets were Owen and

Flora during high school," Willow said. "Not that I think Flora's capable of anything like that, but maybe this Owen guy?"

Easton tipped his head thoughtfully to one side. "Those *were* the two who got the brunt of his attention." He sighed. "Okay, I'll look into their alibis for Credence's time of death, which was eight to ten, not seven," he said with a pointed look at Lou.

She didn't care. She squeezed her fists tighter in celebration. "Thank you."

"You two have done quite a lot of investigating behind my back," Easton said as he stood, stashing away his notebook. Willow and Lou opened their mouths to protest, but he held up a hand to stop them. "I'll check into those alibis." With that, he headed for the door.

"We really appreciate it," Lou said, following him.

He shoved his hands into his pockets. "I wouldn't be a very good detective if I let a murderer wander free, would I?"

Lou waved and said goodbye, glad to have him on their side again. But just as Easton left, Lou got a whole slew of customers, all holding coffee cups. It was as if the crowd from Bean and Button had all come straight over to the bookshop. Lou wasn't complaining, though. Seeing Lou had her hands full, Willow headed home to go for a ride, leaving Lou to her busy, tourist-filled Saturday in the bookshop.

It wasn't until Lou was locking up the store later that day when Willow called.

"I just talked with Easton. He checked into everyone, Lou," she said, the banging of dishes in the background.

Willow was probably just doing her dishes, but the sound reminded Lou of cooking, and she remembered that she'd bought ingredients to cook a special meal tonight. The only problem was, she'd accidentally bought way too much food, used to cooking for two—well, more like three since Ben had such a big appetite.

"Want to come over for dinner?" Lou asked.

"Sure," Willow said. "I could pick up something on my way over."

"Actually," Lou said, "I have ingredients to make something here, and I got way too much."

Willow inhaled sharply. "Really?"

Lou hadn't done a lot of cooking since Ben had passed. It used to be their thing. Other than talking about books, snuggling together while reading books, and running, cooking meals together had been one of their favorite joint pastimes. And for good reason. They were both exceptional chefs, not to mention that their differences had made them the perfect pair in the kitchen. Lou's planning, methodical side kept them on recipe, while Ben's creativity and flair for adventurous tastes took their meals up a notch.

After almost a year without him, she had finally gotten the itch to cook something fun again the other day and had picked up some specific ingredients at the store in preparation.

"Do you need me to pick up anything on my way?" Willow asked, sounding like she was going to run over at the mention of Lou's cooking.

Lou put her coat back on the hook. "Nope. I picked it all up yesterday at the store, actually. I even have a nice white wine that will go great."

"Okay, I'll be over soon," Willow said.

Lou made sure the back door was locked before she and the cats went upstairs. She'd made Willow her own key during her first month in town. That way her friend knew she was always welcome over.

In her kitchen, Lou started prepping the meal. It was one she and Ben had made before, and it had been memorable enough that she was excited to try it again. She got out the fish she'd bought and seasoned it, letting it rest while she prepared the other ingredients.

About ten minutes later, she heard footsteps coming up the

staircase. "Hello, I bring alibis and my taste buds," Willow announced as she entered the apartment.

Lou laughed. "Both are very welcome." She motioned to the small table in the kitchen. "Poured you a glass of wine to sip on while I work." Lou held her own small wineglass up, and Willow clinked hers against it.

"So what are we having?" Willow took a sip and peeked at the list of ingredients.

"Seared halibut in a lemon beurre blanc sauce with sautéed apples, onions, and sweet potatoes." That familiar feeling of warmth spread through Lou as Willow's eyes widened in appreciation. She had missed cooking for people.

Willow settled into a chair at the table. "Well, my thank-you gift will be that I will entertain you with what Easton told me."

Lou nodded, showing that she was listening as she chopped up the sweet potatoes and got those in the skillet.

"So," Willow started, "Timothy said he was driving his daughters around in the minivan. None of them would sleep that night. It's highly unlikely he left three wailing infants alone in the van while he went inside to make it seem like Credence killed himself."

"If the girls actually were in the van," Lou said. "Unless we know where Timothy's wife was, we don't know that for sure."

Willow moved on. "Liza was sneaking around the house, but she went straight to the nail salon after, and she showed Easton her time-stamped receipt. So she's accounted for during the time-of-death window."

Lou stirred the contents of the skillet as it sizzled. "Okay."

Willow went on. "Carol was working a late shift at the hospital. Flora was with her husband, having dinner in Silver Lake for their anniversary. And Owen was online playing a game."

At that, Lou narrowed her eyes.

Willow returned the gesture, telling her she doubted the validity of Owen's alibi as well. "Easton said he wouldn't be able to verify it unless he got a search warrant to look through his computer and that we definitely don't have enough evidence to convince a judge to get him that."

Lou agreed. "Maybe this is where we can help. He might need a warrant to figure out if Owen was really online, but you and I don't. We just need to ask the right person."

"And who would that be?" Willow asked.

"George," Lou said, her eyes sparkling.

CHAPTER 12

George was a twentysomething local who owned the Technology Emporium, an electronics shop she ran out of her tiny home a couple of blocks down the street.

Lou had visited during her second day in town to get security cameras for the shop and had not only been surprised by the amount of stock George had in the small space, but because George was actually a young woman.

In her twenties, George held the self-assured air of someone much older than herself as well as an acute knowledge of all things techie.

Since she'd moved to town, Lou had learned that George's grandparents had raised her. George had been so good at helping her older guardians with technology that she started helping the other technologically challenged people of Button. And when it came time for her to move out of her grandparents' home, she decided she didn't want to leave her small hometown. She'd started her tech company and not only supplied the town with their various electronic needs, but acted as their own personal Geek Squad, helping whenever anyone had a question or had gotten stuck with their devices.

Technically, George's business was an appointment-only establishment, which meant that Lou texted her first to see if she could chat.

> You around tonight? Techie mystery for you.

George had helped Lou out before with technological questions and seemed to love a good head-scratcher.

> Absolutely! Come on by.

Lou surveyed the meal she was just finished preparing. She took a chance and typed,

> Have you eaten dinner yet?

George responded that she hadn't.

> Okay, don't eat. Willow and I are bringing you something, as long as you aren't allergic to fish or dairy.

> I could also come to you so you don't have to pack anything up. I could use a walk to stretch my legs. Been playing a game for the last couple of hours.

Lou smiled as she typed. That was even better.

> Great! Come on over to the bookshop. Willow will wait for you at the front door.

Lou didn't have to repeat any of it for her friend because Willow had snuck into the kitchen, hovering behind Lou, taking tastes of things as she read the texts over her shoulder.

Willow gave a salute and took another sip of her wine before heading downstairs to wait for George. Lou plated the food and was just setting it out on the table when two sets of shoes clomped up the staircase. George's eyes were wide as she took in the small space.

"I've always wondered what it was like up here." Her focus caught on the food. "This looks and smells amazing."

"It'll be ready in just a minute," Lou said, just finishing up the sauce. It was one of those that needed to be prepared right before serving.

George didn't seem to mind the wait, because she got on the floor and played with the cats, who surrounded her as she got on their level.

"This tabby is gorgeous," George said, pulling Jules into her arms for a quick cuddle. "Is it new?"

"She is," Lou answered, but left it at that, knowing Jules's previous owner was likely to count against the beautiful cat. "Okay, I think we're ready." Lou gestured for everyone to take a seat as she put the beurre blanc sauce in a serving bowl and brought it over to the table.

"Thank you," George said, getting up off the floor. "I was just about to make myself a peanut butter and jelly sandwich before you texted. This is way better."

"It's the least I can do to feed you when we need to pick your brain. Wine?" She held the bottle toward George, then pulled it back for a second.

George must've caught the thought process behind the gesture because she laughed and said, "Yes, I'm over twenty-one." She sat up straight, pushing her shoulders back. "I'll have you know I'm twenty-two."

Willow tilted her head and sighed. "I loved twenty-two. That was a great year."

Lou rested her chin on her hands. "I met Ben when I was twenty-two." A huge grin broke over her face. They'd had a creative writing class together at NYU and had hit it off right away.

"Ben?" George sipped at her wine, glancing curiously at Lou as she did so.

"He was my husband," Lou said, pushing through the pain of having to use a past-tense verb. "He passed away last year. It's why I moved out here, actually."

George's eyes went wide as she froze with her fork halfway to her mouth. "I'm so sorry. I had no idea."

Lou shook her head. "Don't be sorry."

"Lou feels that a big part of healing is talking about Ben and letting herself remember the great life they had together, even if it was cut short," Willow explained to George.

The young woman took a bite of her meal but studied Lou as if seeing her in a different light. "That'll teach me to make judgments about people's lives without knowing the complete story," George said.

Lou lowered her eyebrows into a quizzical frown.

"Oh, it's not bad." George waved a hand at her. "It's just, ever since you moved here, I've been thinking how wonderful your life is. You are so nice and seem to be living your dream. It just goes to show you that people are deeper; sometimes they're hiding a lot of pain under the surface."

Lou nodded, sending George a small smile.

"Can I ask how he died?" George grimaced. "I'm sorry. It's none of my business. It's just, I've grown up in this tiny town my whole life, and you hear stories about the crime in big cities."

Lou pushed her food around on her plate. "He died of a heart attack while he was on a run. Just a terribly unlucky thing. He was healthy as a horse. They said sometimes hearts just give out." She took a bite of her halibut. "And you know what? I'd have to say I've experienced more murder in this small town in the three months I've been here than I did in the almost twenty years I lived in New York. I mean, sure, it happened, but I wasn't stumbling onto bodies like I have been here."

George frowned at that statement. "But, I mean, only one of those was a murder. Credence took his own life."

Willow and Lou pressed their lips together into thin lines as they shared a knowing look.

"Wait." George glanced between them. "He *didn't* kill himself?"

Lou raised her palms. "Honestly, we're not sure. But there are definitely things that don't make sense."

They ate a few bites as George digested that information.

"This is amazing, Lou. Thank you." Willow pointed at the dish with her fork and swooned.

"Yeah, it's fantastic," George agreed. She took another bite, swallowed, then said, "So who do you think could've killed Credence, except—I don't know—half the town?" She snorted.

"Believe me, we've tried to winnow it down," Willow said. "We're still not sure if we're searching in the right direction."

"Right now we're interested in Owen Sanchez." Lou took over the story. "We know Owen was one of Credence's biggest targets in high school, and we believe someone from his past might be the killer."

"Why?" George asked.

Lou motioned for Willow to grab the yearbook off the coffee table. She showed it to George, along with the page with Credence's picture and the threatening message.

George's eyes went wide. "And I'm guessing the birthday he just missed was his thirty-eighth?"

"Bingo," Willow said.

"Easton found out that Owen had an alibi, but he said he was online playing a game Friday night between the hours of eight and ten, and Easton can't confirm that on his computer without a search warrant," Lou explained. "Do you know of any other way for us to figure out if that's what he was doing?"

George looked at Lou and then Willow, blinking like she couldn't believe what she was hearing.

Lou readied herself to hear that it was a silly request, but George repeated, "Owen Sanchez?"

"You know him?" Willow asked.

George nodded.

"And is there a way to check to see if he really was on the internet playing a game that night?" Lou asked.

"There's no need," George said. "I can tell you right now that he lied. Owen wasn't online last Friday night."

Lou leaned forward, while Willow sat back in surprise.

"What? How do you know?" Lou asked through a cough.

"He's part of the group I play with online. When we're not in the game, we usually chat on our Discord server. Owen said he couldn't make our regular game time last Friday at six, and he wasn't on the Discord server. That guy logs onto the server and has it running in the background anytime he's on the internet, which is like all day since he works in website management." George put the last bite of food from her plate in her mouth. Once she swallowed, she said, "We were on until eleven. Owen wasn't online that night. He lied to Easton."

"What?" Willow spat out the question.

George sat back, folding her napkin and setting it on the table.

The news swirled around Lou. Or maybe she'd had too many sips of her white wine. She set down her fork and tried to think straight.

"So that means..." Lou started, but couldn't find the right words.

"Owen lying to Easton about where he was during the time of Credence's death definitely doesn't make him seem innocent." Willow summed up for her after finishing the last bite of her meal.

"Agreed," George said, pushing her empty plate forward.

Normally, Lou would've felt happy that both George and Willow had cleaned their plates, proving the food had been yummy. But at that moment, she could only think of the implications this news had on their investigation. In a case that had felt like so many closed doors, this felt like something they could follow—finally an opening.

"Do you know where Owen lives?" Lou asked. "Is he still local, or did he move away?" She realized that the nature of his job meant he could really live anywhere in the country.

"He's in Button still," George said. "In fact, he's also in my Sunday Dungeons and Dragons group, where we meet in person at the library and play for a few hours."

Willow's eyes widened. "Sunday, that's tomorrow."

Lou sat up straight as she got an idea. "Is there any way you could suggest that you hold it here? At the bookshop?"

"Sure. I'll do that right now." George pulled out her phone and started texting.

"And then we can corner the guy and get him to tell the truth about what he was really doing that night," Willow said to Lou conspiratorially as George texted.

Lou didn't know how they would do that just yet, but at least they had until tomorrow to figure out a plan.

"Everyone's in." George set down her phone. "We've actually been talking about moving from the library. We're always getting kicked out earlier than we want since they close at two on Sundays."

"Perfect," Lou said. "Now we just have to come up with a way to get Owen to tell us the truth about where he was on Friday night."

SUNDAY MORNING probably should've dragged by while Lou waited for the Dungeons and Dragons group to show up. But the time actually went by too quickly, in Lou's opinion.

That had a lot to do with the lack of a plan. Without one, they risked wasting the opportunity to question Owen about his alibi.

It wasn't until Silas stumbled in for the day that the idea actually hit her. Silas had his paper rolled and tucked under one arm, as usual. His bowler hat was a little askew that morning, and his fluffy gray eyebrows even wilder than usual.

He grumbled a little as he sat down but puffed out his chest happily when Catnip Everdeen came over and vaulted into his lap.

"I don't know how you do it," Lou said as she watched the cat cuddle up with the old man. "She doesn't like anyone else, but you make her feel comfortable."

He harrumphed. "I don't overcomplicate things," he said. "Other people try too hard to pet her and that annoys her. I just leave her be."

The line "Don't overcomplicate things" stuck out to Lou, and she realized that was exactly what they'd been doing with the whole Owen situation. This wasn't questioning Liza. They didn't need to come up with some elaborate reason to ask him what he was doing last Friday. George was his friend. She could just come out and ask him why he hadn't been at their usual Friday night game.

"Silas, you're a genius," Lou said.

He grumbled something incoherent just as the D and D group walked through the bookshop's front door.

CHAPTER 13

Lou showed the Dungeons and Dragons players to the table she'd set up in the back by the used-books section. George pulled Lou aside as the rest of the group chose their seats and started unpacking their books and dice.

"Any ideas? I'm completely stumped." George rubbed at her eyes as if thinking about what to do had kept her up just as late last night as it had Lou.

Lou nodded. "We're not going to overcomplicate things." When George gave her a questioning glance, she added, "He usually joins you guys on Friday nights. It makes total sense for you to ask him why he wasn't there."

George slapped her palm onto her forehead and chuckled. "I can't believe I didn't think of that before. Right. I can do that." She crossed her fingers. "Let's hope he tells the truth this time."

Lou hoped he did too. One thing was for certain—he couldn't use the online excuse with this group. So they would either hear a different lie, or they would finally get the truth. The only issue was, they really wouldn't have any way of knowing he was lying until Easton could check into it.

Her gaze combed over the group, trying to figure out which

one was Owen. Other than George, there was another person who looked to be in his twenties. He wore a sweatshirt that held the name of a video game console and had floppy blond hair that he kept swiping out of his eyes.

Too young to be Owen, Lou thought to herself, remembering the man in question would've graduated around the same time as Credence, and therefore would've been about the same age as Lou.

There was an older woman with graying hair and dewy skin. The combination made Lou unsure if she was going gray early or if she was older with really great skin. Other than her, the other three men fit the bill. They all appeared to be close to Lou's age. One had a paunchy stomach and little to no hair left on his head. The other two had brown hair. It would've been hard to distinguish them if it wasn't for the fact that one wore a sweatshirt and jeans while the other wore a maroon crushed-velvet suit.

Lou busied herself with organizing the used-book section, staying close by so she could listen in as the group started their game. There was a lot of talk about quests, monsters, and dragons, but a statement from George stuck out from the rest.

"We missed you two Fridays ago, Owen," George said casually.

She focused on the table, only glancing up after a few beats of silence. Lou moved so she had a good view of the entire group in her peripheral vision.

The rest of the group chimed in with similar sentiments. And even though Lou hadn't been able to tell which person George had directed her question toward, the others didn't have any qualms about staring at the man with brown hair in the sweatshirt and jeans.

"What were you up to again?" George asked. "I think you told us but I forgot."

Owen's entire face turned beet red. He grabbed at the collar of his sweatshirt and cleared his throat. "Uh, Friday? Like, two days ago?" His voice cracked even though he was decades past puberty. "What do you mean? I was there."

The paunchy, balding, middle-aged man with a dragon on his T-shirt, frowned up at Owen. "She said two Fridays ago. You said you had plans. What *were* you doing?" Suspicion edged the guy's words.

"I just didn't feel like playing. Okay, Phil?" Owen shrugged, but the motion was jerky.

Phil pressed his lips into an unamused line. "You haven't missed a Friday night in three years. I was actually worried about you for a while, wondered if you shouldn't get out more. But I figured it was none of my business, and then you said you had plans, and I hoped it might be something good."

Lou glanced at George, and they shared a wide-eyed look. This Phil guy was doing all the work for them.

Owen's gaze flicked nervously around the room. He opened his mouth and then closed it again several times, like he was about to say something, but then decided otherwise. Finally, his expression dropped in defeat. George was on the edge of her seat. Lou's fingers pulled back from a book, leaving it teetering on the shelf.

"Look, you don't have to tell us what you were doing." Phil put his hands up and focused on the dice in front of him.

Owen sat back, relaxing. Lou's shoulders fell in defeat. They'd almost had him.

"I don't know. I'd still be interested in what you did that night," George said conversationally. "I want to know what finally got Owen out on a Friday night." She laughed, as did the other members.

The relieved expression Owen wore sank off his face. He swallowed. Everyone in the group stopped what they were doing and turned their attention to him.

"I had a date, okay?" He spat the words out, his cheeks back to their reddened state from earlier.

Lou almost dropped the book she was shelving. A date? That was definitely different from what he'd told Easton.

"Congratulations, man." The guy in the velvet suit slapped him on the back.

But Owen stiffened. "Thanks. I-it was ... thanks." His posture was tight with discomfort.

Something didn't feel right to Lou. He'd already lied to the police. What was to stop him from lying to them now? She narrowed her eyes as she watched him from the corner of her eye.

George seemed to pick up on it, too, because she kept pushing. "That's great, Owen. Anyone we know?"

He sucked in a breath. "Nope. Met her on the internet. Whose turn is it?"

George tilted her head to one side. "Oh no. You can't just leave us with that. How'd the date go? Are you going to see her again?"

"It was fine. I don't think it's going to work, though." He waved a hand.

"Why?" George asked. "If it was fine, why wouldn't you see her again?"

The rest of the group members leaned forward as if they wanted to know the answer as well.

"There just wasn't a connection. We didn't have anything in common," Owen said, brushing it off.

"Wait, then how did you connect online if you had nothing in common?" George asked, frowning at the inconsistencies in his story.

Lou tensed as she waited for his answer.

"Okay, fine," Owen snapped. "You caught me, George. She's not real."

Lou froze. *You caught me?* George had succeeded in getting him to admit his alibi was a lie. Lou waited for the truth.

"So where were you, then, if you weren't on a date?" George asked softly.

"What do you mean?" Owen's voice was sharp, irritated. He

checked over his shoulder to make sure no one else had entered the shop, then said, "I went on the date. She didn't show. I got catfished. When she wouldn't return any of my messages, I stayed up really late that night searching for her online. I found the photo she sent me on a stock-photo site," he admitted quietly.

Lou glanced over just in time to see Owen's head drop forward in defeat.

"Oh, Owen," George whispered. "I'm so sorry. I shouldn't have pushed it."

He groaned. "I'm such a loser. I even gave her money to 'fix her car' so she could drive up from Seattle to meet me," he scoffed.

Lou didn't even want to guess how much that would've cost him, but by the grimace on his face, she guessed it was a significant amount.

"I didn't tell anyone because I was embarrassed." Owen looked at his hands. "I'm sorry, you guys."

In fitting with her old-soul personality, George patted a gentle hand on Owen's back, like a supportive mother might instead of a twentysomething. "Hey, it's okay."

At that moment, Willow rushed into the shop, eyes flitting around the room until she found Lou. She rushed forward, but Lou did, too, meeting her halfway.

"Sorry I'm late. I lost track of time while doing my barn chores." She craned her neck to see around Lou. "What's happened so far?"

Lou wrinkled her nose. "I don't think it was him," she whispered, pushing Willow farther away, toward the front of the shop so they'd be out of earshot. "He lied about being online because he was meeting a date."

Willow's gaze wandered over to where the group sat at the back table. "Oh, that's cute."

Lou flinched. "Not really. He was catfished. The girl never

existed. The person scammed him out of money and never showed for the date."

"Ouch." Willow sucked a breath through her teeth. "Harsh."

"Yeah." Lou glanced over her shoulder at the group.

Jules Purrne had jumped in Owen's lap, rubbing up against his chin. It was as if she knew Owen needed some cheering up. It also occurred to Lou that Jules was used to living with a single man. Owen probably reminded her of Credence, not that she would mention that to Owen.

"Looks like he's got a new friend," Willow said with a smile.

"With perfect timing." Lou watched them.

"You should grab him an adoption application." Willow elbowed Lou.

Lou's heart jumped with hope. Maybe he was looking for a cat, and she could find a home for Jules sooner than she expected. But at the thought of sending the sweet tabby home with the man, doubt crept forward, and she frowned. If she was going to consider him as an adopter, she needed more proof he hadn't been the one to hurt Credence. Not only was that person a murderer, but they'd also locked Jules in a room without food or water.

"I don't know," Lou said, observing as Jules snuggled up even more with Owen. Jules didn't seem like the forgiving kind of feline, and Owen didn't seem to recognize the cat, so Lou felt fairly strongly that he hadn't been the person who'd been in Credence's house and had locked her away.

Still, the knowledge that he'd already lied once made her a little wary of believing him, even though the embarrassing story seemed factual. It could be part of his tactic. Admitting to some-thing embarrassing like that wouldn't be easy, but it would be an excellent cover-up for murder. And if he could do that, he might act as if he didn't recognize Jules to get rid of suspicion.

"Why not? I thought you said you didn't think it was him." Willow snapped Lou out of her thoughts.

"Yeah, but I want to know *for sure* it wasn't him before I trust him with Jules. I wonder if I could get a sample of his handwriting." Lou tapped her fingers against her lips. Before Willow could even respond, Lou snapped her fingers together. "Maybe you were right about that adoption application. I could have him fill it out and say Noah needs to look it over before he can take her home."

Willow dipped her head. "That would work."

Lou plucked an application from the folder she kept by the shop computer and put it behind her back as she walked over to the group. They all glanced up, pausing the move they'd been discussing as she and Willow stopped next to the table.

Eyeing the cat still purring happily in Owen's lap, Lou said, "No pressure, but she is available for adoption. I'm going to leave this application here, just in case." She slid the paper toward Owen. "You can return it to me if you decide you want to fill it out. I can also answer questions you might have about the process."

Owen chewed on his lip for a moment, checking over the adoption paperwork, before nodding. Lou and Willow walked back to the register counter, watching out of the corner of their eyes as the group returned to their game.

The adoption paper sat there throughout the entire morning. Willow left about halfway through the game, citing the need to get OC in the arena for a workout. George, none the wiser of Lou's plot to get a sample of Owen's writing, gave her a discreet thumbs-up as she left.

It reminded Lou that she should feel better about the information they'd learned about Owen's alibi. When she went to break down the table and slide it back into the storeroom, she noticed Owen had taken the adoption application with him. So at least there was that. She wouldn't hold her breath, but it was nice to have a little hope.

"We'll find you a new home soon, Jules," she told the pretty tabby. "I promise."

Lou sighed, knowing that was a promise she could actually keep, unlike all the others she'd made to herself lately. Finding a murderer no one else thought existed—because they believed the victim had killed himself—was turning out to be harder than she thought.

CHAPTER 14

Monday sauntered by like a cat who wants to be petted might walk by their owner, slowly and purposefully. Lou had been productive, deep cleaning the shop and dusting all the shelves.

Noah had come by with a sewn fleece bed for the recent addition to the shop, smiling as he pet Jules. He and his daughter, Marigold, sewed a bed for each of the fosters in Lou's shop. Small fleece beds littered the bookshelves and quiet corners of the store, giving the cats soft places to nap and providing them with something to bring home when they were adopted.

Lou spent some of the afternoon thinking of Catsby and wondering how he was doing in his new home. She hoped Hannah and Sage would come in soon to give her an update.

The slow pace of the day made Lou feel better about closing early again. Once she closed the shop, Lou walked up to the high school. She had a meeting with Evelyn to start the book ordering process and needed to go through that last box of books before they did so.

Evelyn had emailed that she had to run her grandson over to Silver Lake after school for a soccer game but that she'd be back in time for their meeting, so it did not surprise Lou when the library was empty and dark when she arrived. She flicked on the lights and went straight to the back room.

It only took Lou half an hour to go through the last box from Carol's donation and add the titles to the list she'd started last week. While she worked, she couldn't help but think more about that yearbook.

She was contemplating whose it might be when someone said, "Hello," behind her.

Lou shrieked, having been so lost in her thoughts that she hadn't heard anyone enter the back room.

"Just me," Evelyn said, putting both her hands up to show she wasn't a threat. She laughed. "I should've known better than to sneak up on you. I used to startle the kids who would hang out in here back in the day."

"No worries," Lou said. She got up from where she was seated, cross-legged, on the floor, dusting off her pants. "I just finished with the list."

Lou held it out toward Evelyn who took it and looked it over as she walked out into the library toward the circulation desk.

"Perfect, I'll show you how to start the ordering process, and I can be here with you for"—she checked her watch—"another half hour before I have to get back to pick up the littlest grand-daughter from ballet." Evelyn motioned for Lou to take a seat since she knew she was leaving soon.

Lou slid into the chair in front of the computer and looked over at Evelyn. "Hey, before we get started, I wonder if I can ask a question about Credence."

Evelyn nodded.

"Did you see any baked goods sitting on his front porch by his door?" Lou wondered if the woman could've possibly even been the one to bake them for him.

Evelyn shook her head. "I didn't. I'm sorry."

So it hadn't been her to leave the plate of treats on his porch.

Lou sighed. "Do you have any idea who might've dropped off cookies for Credence's birthday?"

"No. Most people on our street avoided his house at all costs." Suddenly Evelyn snapped her fingers, giving Lou hope. "You know. Maybe that's what that woman was doing. What if she'd been sneaking around so she could drop off cookies." Evelyn smiled like it all made sense.

Lou experienced a very opposite emotion. She turned her attention back to the book ordering. "Okay, if you get me started, I can take it from there today."

Evelyn did, and they'd placed over a hundred books in their cart before she had to leave to pick up her granddaughter. Lou added a few more after Evelyn was gone, checking the hand-written list she'd made before adding each to the cart, to make sure they didn't duplicate titles.

"This is a pleasant sight," Willow said when she poked her head into the library an hour later. "Are you sure you don't want to take over for Evelyn when she retires at the end of the year?"

Lou shook her head as she laughed. "I love books, but I don't know if I can say the same about teenagers. I might have to leave that to you."

"Yeah, they can be difficult sometimes, but I sure love those weirdos." Willow smiled fondly.

"Plus, I would need a whole different degree," Lou added.

Willow waved those worries away like they were as easy to get as picking up more bread at the store. She glanced over her shoulder, and it was then Lou noticed Willow's braid was askew and she had puffy circles under her eyes. She looked frazzled again.

"Hey, you doing okay?" Lou asked, concern edging her tone.

Willow scratched at her forehead as she surveyed the library. "Yeah, I'm just … missing my schedule for the festival. I swear I just had it. I thought I'd check to see if I left it in here. I can go print another one in my classroom, but my computer is so old and slow, it's easier to search for the one I lost. Plus, I have to go check on the students in the lounge. They're having a festival meeting and I need to get back."

"Can I help?" Lou asked. "I'm done here." She slid out of the tall chair behind the circulation desk, leaving the order on the screen for Evelyn like she'd asked.

Willow's eyes brightened. "Would you? That would be great. I know for sure there's a schedule in Flora's office. I put it on her desk. If you would just go in there, grab it, and make a copy, that would be an enormous help. I don't think anyone's in the office, but use this." She handed over a ring of keys, holding on to one specific key. "Flora's office will be closed, but not locked."

"I'm allowed to go into her office?" Lou asked.

"Yeah." Willow waved a hand. "She keeps confidential stuff locked up. You're fine."

Lou took the ring, careful to keep the office key separate. "And I'll bring the copy to you in the student lounge?" She tried to remember where that was in the large maze of a school.

"That would be great." Willow waved over one shoulder as she headed down the hall.

Keys jangling in her right hand, Lou followed the signs pointing to the main office. She thought being here so much over the past week would've meant she felt less lost in the maze of hallways, but it appeared not to be the case.

Finally, making it to the office, Lou unlocked the door and entered the dark space. She walked through to Flora's office, behind the secretary and registrar's desks. It was unlocked, like Willow had said it would be, and she flicked on the light, eyes poring over the desk.

A single piece of paper with the schedule of events sat on top of her desk. Lou plucked it off and turned back into the office to make a copy. The lights of the copy machine flashed as it cranked out a duplicate and delivered it, warm, to Lou's waiting hands.

She was setting the original back onto Flora's desk when her eyes caught on something written on the desk calendar underneath.

Two weeks from today, on the seventh of April, was a hand-written note encircled by a heart. *Our anniversary*. It stood out to Lou not only because April seventh had also been her and Ben's anniversary date, but also because hadn't Flora told Easton that her alibi two Fridays ago was that she was out with her husband for their anniversary dinner?

Lou knew life often got in the way and couples couldn't always celebrate on the actual day, but this was almost a month early. Her heart rate increased as the realization that Flora might've lied about her alibi grew as a possibility in her mind.

In a normal case, Easton would've corroborated all the alibis and checked into their validity. But he'd only asked the suspects in this case as a favor to Lou and Willow. It didn't sound like he'd done much more digging than the act of asking, especially in Owen's case, which had indeed been a lie. What if Owen hadn't been the only one to lie?

Just as Lou moved to set the schedule back on Flora's desk, one in each hand, something sparkly caught her eye. It was a card that said *Best Principal Ever!* in lime-green glitter, propped up on the corner of her desk, behind a picture of Flora and her husband. Lou gasped. The spec of glitter she'd seen on Credence's cheek the day she discovered his body had been the same lime-green color.

Lou's stomach churned as she realized they hadn't really taken Flora seriously as a suspect. She'd been so easy to dismiss because, even if she was bullied extensively by Credence back in the day, she seemed so successful now.

But Lou should've known better.

Sometimes a person can appear happy, seem like they have it all together on the outside, but be a broken mess inside. Take her, for example. She thought back to how surprised George had been the other night at dinner when she heard Lou had gone through such a devastating loss. *Sometimes they're hiding a lot of pain under the surface,* George had said about people.

Clicking a quick picture of the desk calendar and the sparkly card with her phone, Lou set the festival schedule back onto Flora's desk. She walked in a daze through the halls to the student lounge.

Willow smiled as she saw her enter, but her expression immediately fell. Walking over, she asked, "What's wrong? You look pale, like you might throw up."

Lou swallowed. It wasn't nausea, but there was definitely something in her throat she didn't want to come out. Words. She knew how much Willow respected and idolized her principal. Would she even believe Lou when she brought up the possibility of Flora as a suspect?

Lou had to trust her friend. She pulled out her phone. "Willow, I think we were wrong to discount Flora so quickly." She showed her the two pictures. "She obviously lied to Easton about her alibi, and look, this is the same lime-green glitter I saw on Credence's skin." After she was finished speaking, Lou studied her friend, observing how her words would hit her.

Willow puffed out her cheeks, but then she said, "You're right. This doesn't bode well for Flora. We need to do some major digging to see if you're right."

Lou agreed, but as good as it felt to have her friend believe her, to be on her side, Lou got a terrible feeling in her gut. This high school building was already a confusing maze, but what if it held more sinister secrets within its walls?

CHAPTER 15

"Okay," Willow said, frowning as she appraised the students at work in the lounge. "They're here for another half an hour, and then I can head home. You should come with me, and we can take this evidence next door to Easton. He'll have to get involved if he hears Flora lied about her alibi, right?"

Lou nodded, hoping she was. "Do you need any help in here?" she asked.

Willow gestured to the students painting a sign in the corner. "We have it under control if there's more you need to do in the library. I can come find you."

There was, so Lou took her up on the offer. She wanted to clean up the mess she made in the storage room. Evelyn had interrupted her, and she'd left books in haphazard piles. She should at least move them to the shelf so they weren't in Evelyn's way if she needed to walk back there.

Lou moved the books to one of the industrial metal shelves in the back so they were up off the floor. She broke down the cardboard boxes they'd come in and had those in a pile to throw in the recycling bin. She'd ask Willow where that was.

But as she set the last flattened box on the floor and went to grab the stack of them, the toe of her shoe hit the corner of the top box and it went skittering across the floor and under one of the wooden bookshelves pushed up against the wall.

Lou went to retrieve it, but a confusing sight stopped her. She tipped her head to the right as she studied the large piece of cardboard. It had almost completely disappeared underneath the bookshelf. Only one small corner stuck out from under the shelf, but the wall should've stopped it.

Blinking at what must be an optical illusion, Lou knelt to inspect it.

She was met with what looked like a regular old bookshelf until she noticed old scratches leading in long lines to the right of the furniture's wooden feet on the concrete floor.

Which meant—Lou leaned closer—someone had shoved this bookshelf aside more than once.

She moved to the left side and placed her feet on the wood. Then she pushed. It took a moment, but finally it slid.

Behind it was an opening in the wall. Lou couldn't tell if it was a room or a passageway since the space beyond the wall was pitch black, so she brought out her phone from her pocket and turned on the flashlight function. She gasped as the light illuminated a much bigger space than what she'd imagined. It was a room, and it had to be at least thirty feet square.

Lou slid through the opening. Using her phone's beam, she located a switch on the wall and clicked it on. A light on the ceiling above illuminated the space, and she turned off her phone's flashlight, returning it to her pocket.

It was then that Lou remembered Willow's tour of the high school during her first visit. This must've been one of the civil defense shelters she'd mentioned that had been built into the school during the Cold War. Now it was being used as some forgotten old storage room.

There were stacks of old gym mats, dusty towers of boxes, and a shelf full of old Button High yearbooks. There were a few empty cans of Tab soda in one corner and an empty plastic Squeeze It drink container in another. No one had been here in decades by the look of things.

On the wall there were a few posters stuck to the brick with hardened chewing gum. One poster was for a popular nineties boy band and the other was of a horse running in a green field.

Nostalgia filled Lou. She and Willow had a very similar setup in Willow's treehouse back at her parents' house during their teenage years.

The posters weren't the only things stuck to the wall, though. A piece of lined notebook paper with the title *Boys We Think Are Cute* hung lower on the wall, complete with yearbook pictures— Lou guessed they'd been cut from one of the many behind her. Lou almost laughed, but any sense of a smile slid off her face as she got close enough to recognize the last thing that had been hung on the wall. It was a piece of paper much like the one that held the pictures of cute boys, but this one held the title of *People We Hate.* And this page held only one picture.

Credence Crowley.

The eyes had been poked out of the photo with what looked like a tack. Lou shivered at the sight.

It was the same picture of Credence that Noah had pointed out in the very first set of yearbooks they'd looked through for their Spring Fling prep. Studying the list of cute boys with a fresh eye now that she'd seen the desecrated picture of Credence, Lou realized the handwriting was familiar. She couldn't tell for sure if it was the same as the yearbook, but she snapped a picture with her phone so she could check when she got home.

What was this? A hideaway for a killer? No, it screamed teenage girl. This was a hangout for a high school girl, maybe a few, given the use of the word *we* on all the signs.

This had to be the sanctuary of teenage girls who'd hated Credence Crowley enough for him to make the wall next to the most important things in their lives: horses, boy bands, and their crushes. This was some sort of time capsule.

The sound of Willow calling out Lou's name snapped her out of her time traveling.

"I'm in here," she called, moving closer to the opening.

The storage room door swung open just as Lou poked her head out of the thin opening between the bookshelf and the wall.

"Over here," she said when Willow stepped inside.

Willow jumped as she noticed Lou. "What are you doing?"

"I found a secret room." She beckoned Willow to follow her. For some reason, it felt like something that would be easier to believe if her friend could see it.

"Oh wow," Willow said as she slid through the entrance behind Lou. She glanced around. "Apparently, this was a teenage girl hangout back in the day."

"Not just any teenage girls." Lou waved for her friend to follow so she could get a closer look. "Does any of this look familiar?"

Willow squinted at the posters. "I think I had that exact same horse poster in the treehouse, and oh my gosh, I thought Derek was so dreamy." She pointed to a boy in the poster who looked like he'd just stepped out of the shower, he'd used so much gel in his slicked-back hair.

Lou scratched at her nose as the dust tickled her nostril. "Nobody's been in here for decades, I'd wager. And the girls who made this their hangout had to be around the same age as us."

"Omigosh." Willow clapped her hand over her mouth as she pointed with her other hand at the list of cute boys and their pictures. "Easton is on this list." She barked out a laugh. "He's going to die when I tell him."

"More importantly, look at this." Lou tried to focus her friend's attention on the picture of Credence with his eyes poked out.

Willow leaned in close to get a better view. "Whoever hung

out in here did not like Credence." Her eyes flashed with understanding. "We have to tell Easton."

"Agreed," Lou said. "This could be even more evidence that it was Flora. She went here at the same time as him and Easton."

Excitement filled her as she realized the detective would have to believe them now. This was too much evidence for him to look past. But just as they were pushing the bookshelf back into place and placing the flattened cardboard box on the stack of others, Lou got a call. It was Noah.

"Hey, what's up?" she asked.

"I'm here at the clinic with Owen. He's decided to adopt Jules." Noah's voice was warm, and she could picture his face lit up, pulled into that dimpled smile of his.

"Oh." A wave of surprise hit her, and it took her a moment to regain her focus. "He came to you?"

"Well, we've known each other for a long time, and he tried going by the bookstore, but you weren't there, so he tried me, knowing we were working together on the adoptions. I'm looking at his application, and it all seems in order." Noah paused. When he spoke again, his voice was quieter. "He's really excited and would like to see if he could bring Jules home today. I'm not sure if you're close by. I told him it would depend on what your plans were tonight."

"Oh, I"—she glanced over at Willow, who waved at her and mouthed *go*—"I'm just at the high school, but I could be there in about ten minutes."

"That's great." Noah covered the receiver, but Lou heard a muffled, "She'll meet us there in a few."

"Noah," she said, waiting until he returned his attention to the phone.

"Yeah?"

"Bring Owen's application with, would you? I'd love to look it over too." She mostly wanted to see if the handwriting matched. The secret room might very well be a link, but she didn't want to discount any other suspects, and Owen was not yet completely off her list.

"Will do," he said. "See you in a few."

When Lou hung up with Noah, she turned to Willow. "Okay, I'm just going to meet Owen and Noah, finalize the adoption, and then I can meet you at your place for dinner so we can talk to Easton together."

Willow nodded. "Sounds good. That'll give me some time to finish up here and do my barn chores."

"Okay," Lou said.

They parted ways and headed off to take care of things before they could return to the case, hopefully, with a detective fully on their side this time.

CHAPTER 16

Lou jogged back to the bookstore, her excitement growing with each step as she approached Whiskers and Words. Jules would have a new home. She was so happy for the cat, though she was a little sad to see her go so soon. She'd barely gotten to know her.

Noah and Owen stood outside the bookstore when she arrived. Owen held a brand new cat carrier and bounced on his toes excitedly.

"Hey," Lou said, slowing to a stop as she rounded the corner. "Sorry that took me a minute." She swiped at her slightly sweaty forehead.

"No problem," Owen said. "I'm sorry to bug you after hours. I just thought about it all day, and by the time I made up my mind, you were closed, but I couldn't stop thinking about her, and I took the off chance that Noah could help. Which he did." Owen beamed.

"I've been closing a little early on Mondays," Lou explained. "I'm glad you talked to Noah. Here, let's go inside."

Noah handed Lou the application as he walked past her while she held open the door for the two to enter. Scanning it, Lou could tell right away this was no match for the writing in the old year-book she'd found. It was barely legible, scratched out in mostly capital letters, thin and jagged instead of the large, bubbly writing from the yearbook. She knew handwriting changed over the years, so she wasn't looking for an exact match, but this wasn't even in the same realm.

The last bit of doubt about letting Jules go with Owen washed away as she appraised the application, acting like she was interested in the information he'd written instead of focusing on the sample of his handwriting.

A few of the cats were already stretching and jumping off the bookshelves or extricating themselves from a warm bed to come say hello. Lou didn't see Jules, so she made kissing noises and called her name, having found her to be very responsive. It must've been how Credence had called her.

Lou heard a trilling meow that sounded a lot like a hello, followed by soft little footsteps on the wood floors. But she also heard a loud sneeze, followed quickly by another. She frowned, rounding a bookshelf to find Purrt Vonnegut sitting in the middle of the aisle cleaning his face. Lou thought she might've imagined the sneezing until he did it again.

"Jules is over here," Noah called from across the bookstore.

Lou hesitated and then turned her attention toward getting Jules set up with Owen. She could worry about Purrt after that.

"Okay, let's get this little lady ready to go home with you," Lou said, turning back to Owen and Noah.

Owen left half an hour later with Jules tucked safely in the brand new crate. He had a litter box and a basket of toys waiting for her at home, along with at least three cat beds, from what Lou could count from their conversation. Noah crossed his arms contentedly as he watched Owen leave.

"I think they're going to be very happy together. Owen's a great guy. Always has been." He shoved his hands into his pockets.

Lou agreed with that assessment of Owen now that she'd spent a little more time with him, and that she could see his handwriting was definitely not a match for that of Credence's potential murderer.

"Before you go, do you think you could look at Purrt?" Lou asked. "He was sneezing earlier, and now that I think about it, he's been a little lethargic over the past few days. I'll pay for the exam fee. I'm just worried about the little guy."

Noah's mouth pulled into his usual laid-back, dimpled smile. "Of course. I thought I heard a wet sneeze while we were helping Owen with Jules. Let me look at him." He stopped and turned around. "And there's no way I'm charging you for this. You do me so many favors with keeping these guys here instead of making me take them to the humane society. It's the least I can do."

Another half an hour later, and Noah had diagnosed Purrt with having just a *little cold.* "Sometimes this happens if they're stressed or dealing with a big change." Noah leaned back on his heels.

"He has been upset about Jules," Lou said, glad the source of his stress was off to her forever home now.

Even though Jules was gone, Noah gave Lou the name and brand of a supplement he liked, to give the cat's immune system a little boost while he was fighting off the cold, and she thanked him profusely.

It wasn't until he left, Lou remembered she was supposed to go to Willow's for dinner so they could tell Easton about Flora's lie and the secret room they'd found in the library storage room. Peering down at Purrt, though, she decided he needed to be her priority. The local pet store was only open for another half an hour, and she really wanted to get that supplement for him tonight.

Texting Willow, she explained about the sick cat and asked if she could grab a rain check for dinner tonight.

Sounds good. I got stuck here at school for a little longer, so I'm just now on my way home. I'll talk to Easton and let you know what he says. Good luck with Purrt!

Lou thanked her friend and locked up, walking a few blocks down to the small strip mall where the pet store was located. She found the supplement Noah had recommended and bought two just in case the cold spread to any of the other cats. When she got back home, she brought Purrt upstairs with her and left the rest of the pack downstairs, where they were all cozy and asleep in various places in the bookshop.

She gave Purrt his first dose of the supplement and cuddled up with him after dinner while she read. It was super cozy until the cat sneezed, and wet droplets scattered across the page of her book.

"Oh, Purrt." She pouted as she stared down at his pathetic little face. "Those supplements should kick in soon, and you'll be feeling better before you know it. I'm so sorry you were stressed enough that you caught a little kitty cold, though." She gave him a gentle face massage, and he purred. But even that was sad because he was stuffed up, and his breath rattled as it passed through his little pink nose.

It wasn't until Purrt left her lap a while later that Lou remembered she needed to check the handwriting from the secret room against the threatening yearbook. She moved over to where the yearbook sat on her coffee table, pulling up the picture on her phone.

Frowning, Lou didn't see the automatic match she hoped she would as she held the *Cute Boys* picture up to the *Most likely to be murdered* text in the yearbook. While they were similar, there was a slant to the yearbook writing that made it clear it came from a different person. Lou swiped back to the previous picture on her phone. It was the desk calendar from Flora's office.

With a gasp, Lou flicked to the picture she was just looking at. After going back and forth twice more, Lou knew she'd found a handwriting match, just not where she'd been searching for one at first. The handwriting from the *Cute Boys* list was an exact match for Flora's desk calendar.

Even though that should've felt like a significant discovery, Lou couldn't help but feel more puzzled as she stared down at the yearbook page. If Flora hadn't written this, who had? Who was the other person who'd hung out in that room?

Lou checked her text messages, but there wasn't anything from Willow yet. It was getting pretty late, and she still hadn't heard anything. She hoped the conversation with Easton had gone well. They needed him on their side.

THE FOCUSED LOVE AND ATTENTION—AND the supplement Noah had prescribed—seemed to do the trick for Purrt, because he was much perkier in the morning. He sneezed a few times while Lou was getting ready, but nothing compared to the amount he'd sneezed last night. His nose seemed clearer as well.

Lou scooped him into her arms and hugged him tight before she went down to the bookshop. "Why don't you hang out here for the day?" she suggested. "The peace and quiet might be just what you need." She gave him his second dose of his supplement and then went downstairs.

The other cats, alternately, seemed starved for interaction, and they all crowded around her as she made her way into the bookshop.

"Sorry, friends. Purrt needed a little extra quiet time last night." Normally they all came upstairs with her at night, but she knew they were just as cozy in the bookshop.

After feeding the cats and cleaning their many litter boxes, she made herself a coffee and opened the shop. The morning was foggy, unlike the beautiful blue skies and sun they'd been experiencing as of late. It made Lou want to snuggle up with a book and read, a feeling she gave in to when she didn't have a customer for the first half an hour.

She was curled up with her coffee, a couple of cats, and a book when a woman came inside and scanned the shop.

"Hello, how can I help you?" Lou asked, a little embarrassed to be discovered relaxing on the job, even if it was her store.

The woman was in a gray suit with heels and the smoothest bun Lou had ever seen. She wore red lipstick, and her eyeliner application was on a par with professional makeup artists.

"Hi." The moment the woman's gaze landed on Lou, the searching scowl she'd been wearing disappeared, leaving behind a genuine smile. "I'm Tiffany. Timothy's wife." She held her hand out to shake and Lou stood, reaching out to take it.

The woman had one heck of a grip, and Lou remembered Forrest telling her Mrs. Davis was a lawyer in Kirk.

"Yes. Hello. It's so great to meet you." Lou tried to keep her grip firm, resisting the urge to let her hand crumple under the weight of Tiffany's grip. "What can I help you with today?"

"I just wanted to come in and thank you for the books you brought the girls. It was so thoughtful of you, and we're just so grateful to have the bookshop in town." The polished woman teared up as she talked. "We've been going through such a hard time getting them to sleep lately, and the knowledge that we have extra copies of their favorite book is great peace of mind. That Saturday night two weeks ago was awful without it."

Lou tilted her head sympathetically. "Timothy seemed like he hadn't gotten a wink of sleep when he came in to buy the book the next morning."

Tiffany groaned. "Neither of us did. It was such a one-eighty from the night before too. Friday night, they were all asleep at the same time, and Timothy even got to slip away and see his friends for poker." Tiffany watched Lou's expression crumple into a frown, so she started explaining. "He really needs things like that. I get to leave most days for work, so it's good for him to get out every once in a while."

But Lou hadn't needed the explanation. The reason she was frowning was because that was a different alibi than he'd given Easton. He'd said he was driving one of his daughters around who couldn't sleep. But from what Tiffany was saying, all three of the girls fell asleep that night.

So the question was, why didn't Timothy want Easton to know he went out to play poker with his friends?

Maybe because it would put him near the scene of the crime. Or maybe because he didn't actually go to poker. What if he told Tiffany one thing but actually went to get even with Credence for the car issues they'd had?

"Oh, that's nice." Lou tried to school her expression back to something pleasant. "Is that a usual thing for him?"

"He used to have a standing poker game each Friday with his friends before the girls came along. This is the first one he's been able to make since they were born. With three of them, we usually need all hands on deck during the nighttime routine." She grinned. "Anyway, I just wanted to tell you thank you so much."

"Oh, you're very welcome." Lou forced her lips into a smile. "I can't wait to see the girls running around the shop, picking out books to read on their own someday."

Tiffany nodded. "It'll happen before any of us are ready, I'm sure." She waved to Lou and walked out the door.

As nice as the encounter was meant to be, Tiffany's visit left Lou with a cold, clammy feeling. Just as she'd done with Flora, it seemed that she'd discounted Timothy as a suspect too soon. It appeared he could be a kind, nurturing father, but he might also be out for revenge. Because he'd obviously lied about his alibi to at least Easton, but maybe he'd also lied to his wife.

CHAPTER 17

Lou texted Willow right after Tiffany left the bookshop.

> How'd talking to Easton go last night? I think I have something to add. Flora wasn't the only one who lied to him about her alibi.

But Lou didn't expect a reply anytime soon. Willow usually left her phone in her classroom when she was teaching, and during the spring, her classes often ventured out to the greenhouses right away. She might not check it until lunch at the earliest, probably not until after school.

Lou had her last meeting with Evelyn today to complete the order, so she could swing by Willow's classroom before that to see how everything had gone.

Worry and excitement danced through her, creating a tingly, odd sensation that wouldn't go away all day.

Lou closed the shop early again, as she'd been trying out on Mondays and Tuesdays. She was interested in studying her weekly sales numbers to see what kind of impact the early closing would have but felt optimistic it would be fine.

Before she left for the high school, Lou went upstairs to check on Purrt. He'd been curled in a ball, asleep in the sun on her couch, when she'd checked on him at lunchtime.

But apparently, all the pampering she'd been giving him over the past twelve hours had gone to his head because he refused to take the next dose of his supplement when Lou tried to give it to him before she left.

"You're turning into a real diva, aren't you, Purrt?" Lou put her hand on her hip and checked the time. "I can give it one more try, but then I have to get going."

Purrt wouldn't take the supplement, so she would just have to leave it and try again when she got home after her meeting. She walked up to the school, moving fast so she would make it in time to see Evelyn.

Before her attempts to give Purrt his supplement, she would've had time to go visit with Willow prior to her meeting, but now she would have to leave it for after. Evelyn had to get her grandson to soccer practice and only had a limited amount of time.

On the way down the hallway to the library, Lou spotted Flora walking farther down the hall. Lou's posture stiffened, and her mind immediately latched on to a plan to get her talking about her anniversary. They had the same anniversary date after all. It wouldn't be tough to strike up a conversation.

But Lou didn't have much time, and she didn't want to waste any of Evelyn's, knowing how busy the woman was.

Plus, if Flora really had killed Credence, it probably wasn't smart of Lou to admit that she'd been snooping around in her office. Sure, Lou had gone in to run an errand for Willow, but she'd snooped nonetheless.

Chewing on her lip, Lou decided not to try. She didn't know what Willow had said to Easton yet. Maybe he was already handling the situation, bringing Flora in for questioning and the lot. She would have to find out later.

Quickening her pace, Lou turned the last corner to the library. Evelyn was waiting at the computer. She smiled as Lou entered.

"I was just checking over the books you added after I left last night. They all look great. I had a few questions. I noted the ones I'd like to go through." Evelyn waved a notepad in the air.

Lou took a seat next to her this time, letting her stay behind the computer.

Once they'd gone through the books Evelyn had questions about, and she had the chance to veto a few, knowing better than Lou that they weren't quite suitable for young adults but leaned more toward the adult end of the spectrum, they submitted the order.

"Phew. That feels good." Evelyn turned to Lou.

Lou nodded. "You're leaving quite the gift for the next librarian. Do you know who that's going to be yet?"

"Not yet," she said. "There are a few internal candidates who have expressed interest, and I'm sure some out-of-district folks will apply as well. They probably won't interview until May." Evelyn reached down and patted her knee with a wince. "Though, I'm selfishly hoping they hire a little earlier than that. I'm not sure this knee is going to make it all the way to the summer before it needs surgery."

"That's not selfish," Lou said. "You've been here thirty years. You should ask if an earlier hire is a possibility. Maybe they can use the time you're recovering to try out different substitutes and see if anyone's a good fit."

Lou thought about Willow's joke about her taking over. As much as she loved the time she'd spent in the school library, she knew her bookshop full of rescue cats was exactly where she belonged.

"That's not a bad idea," Evelyn said, checking her watch. "Well, I'd better pack up before I need to be off."

"Can I show you something quickly after you gather your things?" Lou asked.

Evelyn bobbed her head, listening as she stuck her arms into a light spring jacket.

"Last night, while I was cleaning up in the storeroom, I found a secret room hidden behind the eastern wall. Did you know about it?"

"A secret room?" Evelyn's eyes grew wide. "No."

Lou's head kicked back in surprise. She assumed a librarian would've known all the secrets of the building after being there for thirty years.

"But now that you say that, a few things over the years make a lot more sense." She tipped her head to one side.

"Like what?" Lou asked.

"Well, student helpers of mine would often disappear back there for long periods of time. Or students would go back for something and when I would go to find them, they'd be gone. I guess I assumed I just hadn't seen them sneak out, but maybe they were hiding in there."

Evelyn limped after Lou as she led her back to the room. Lou used her shoulder to shove aside the bookshelf. The librarian's eyes went wide as she stepped through the opening and scanned the secret storeroom.

"Yep, it definitely seems like someone spent a lot of time in here," Evelyn said.

"Who were the students who disappeared back here? Do you remember?" Lou asked eagerly.

Evelyn puffed out her cheeks. "Oh, boy. That's like asking me to name every book I've ever read. There were so many of them through the years."

Lou tried a different tactic. "Was Flora ever one of them?"

Evelyn raised her eyebrows. "Flora Henning? Yes. Back then she was Flora Lucas, of course. But she was a student helper of mine for two years in a row, I believe."

Lou squeezed her fingers into a fist as things clicked together. Flora lied about her alibi. She was bullied ruthlessly in high school by Credence, according to everyone who'd gone to school with them. And she had access to the secret room where there were clues pointing to Credence's killer.

"Do you know who she used to hang out with?" Lou asked, trying to figure out who the other part of *we* had been from the signs.

Evelyn only shook her head. "She was a bit of a loner."

Lou thought about that. Maybe Flora had made up friends. Could she have changed her handwriting in the yearbook on purpose? That might be the kind of deeply hurt person who needed to come back as the principal to prove she could conquer the terrible past she'd had there. That kind of person definitely seemed like someone to hold a grudge against the bully who'd made her life so difficult.

"Oh, my. Whoever spent time in here wasn't a fan of Mr. Crowley's," Evelyn said as she noticed the picture of him stuck to the wall.

"You remember when Credence was here?" Lou asked tentatively.

Evelyn tsked, but nodded. "That boy was trouble from the very beginning. It wasn't much of a surprise, given the family he came from. Mean-spirited people, all of them. I doubt that boy knew anything but malice from the day he was born."

"Did he ever come into the library?" Lou asked.

Evelyn snorted. "No. Thank goodness. But my friend Betsy was his bus driver for years until he got his license. Said he was an absolute terror, especially to the girls who rode the bus."

That sounded about right. Lou wondered if Flora had been one of those girls. "Is Betsy still in Button?" Lou asked, thinking it might be really helpful to speak with her.

"Yep," Evelyn said. "She retired last year, but she still lives over on Stitch Street. She's really gotten into gardening over the past year. Our retirements will look very different. Mine will be full of my grandchildren, while hers is full of short people of a very different variety." When Lou cocked her head, Evelyn said, "Gnomes. The woman's gone gnome crazy."

Lou laughed.

"But once my schedule settles down a bit more, we're supposed to travel together. See the world." Evelyn smiled.

"That sounds nice," Lou said.

Lou wanted to turn the subject back to Credence, but Evelyn shouldered her purse and said, "I've got to head out. Thank you for all of your help, Lou. Will you turn the lights out on your way out?"

"I'll walk out with you," Lou said, following Evelyn out of the secret room. She shoved the bookshelf back in place, hiding the preserved room from the rest of the school. From the library, she went to Willow's classroom, thankful she was getting the hang of the route from the library to the science hall and wasn't getting lost anymore.

Willow was inside, sitting at her desk, her hair a frazzled mess from her hands combing through it.

"Hey, how's it going?" Lou asked warily as she set down her bag and walked forward.

"Ugh. Everything's falling apart." Willow motioned to a mountain of papers on her desk. "Flora looked at the schedule, and I missed three whole activities. I have to rework everything to fit them in. On top of that, I gave a big test in all of my classes today and wanted to get them graded and turned back to the students, but I'm not sure that's going to happen anytime soon."

Lou felt bad moving past that, so as much as she wanted to ask her friend about Easton and what he'd said the night before, she said, "How can I help?"

Willow glanced up, her expression soft and thankful. "Okay, first we need to focus on the schedule. I've been staring at it for an hour and can't seem to see a way to make it work. Do you mind putting that super detail-oriented mind of yours to work on it while I grade some of these tests?"

Lou nodded and got started. She scratched her head at first, seeing the conundrum Willow was in. She isolated all the problems, working solutions out like potential moves on a chessboard. Some worked, and others didn't, but she had a version she thought might be the one.

She was almost done with the revised schedule when Willow gasped. "Oh, Lou. I just saw your text from this morning." She groaned. "I totally forgot to ask Easton last night. He wasn't there when I got home, and then I did my barn chores and collapsed on the couch. I didn't even make it to my bed last night."

Lou waved a hand. "It's okay. Don't worry about it. We would have new information to tell him anyway, so maybe it's for the best that you didn't."

"What new information?" Willow leaned forward.

"Nope." Lou pointed at her friend. "You finish grading those tests, and I'm going to finish this schedule, and then we can talk about the case."

"Deal." Willow focused on her tests.

It was only another twenty minutes before they were both done.

"Okay, so tell me what you learned." Willow rested her elbows on the desk in front of her.

"Timothy lied about where he was that Friday night." Lou waited for Willow's reaction before going on. Once she sat back and gasped, Lou added, "He said he was driving the girls around because they wouldn't sleep, but his wife told me they were all asleep that night, so Timothy went out to play poker with his friends."

"Why wouldn't he just tell Easton that?" Willow wondered.

"Maybe because he actually wasn't there, and he knows the guys he plays poker with would've told the truth." Lou crossed her arms in front of her.

"Oh, man." Willow whistled. "Now we really have to talk to Easton."

"That's not even all of it, though." Lou let her arms drop to her sides. "When I was just talking to Evelyn, she mentioned Flora was one of her student helpers and that she could've been the one to find the secret room. The handwriting on the cute boys sign matches the writing on her calendar in her office. A calendar which clearly shows that Flora's alibi is a lie. Her anniversary isn't until next month."

Willow tapped the pen she'd been using for grading on her desk as she thought. "So, what do we do now? Do you want me to text Easton?"

Lou wet her lips. "That might be a good idea. Just in case you two don't get home at the same time tonight again."

Willow pulled out her phone. "Hey, Easton," she narrated as she typed. "Timothy and Flora lied to you about where they were on the night Credence died. There's also a secret room in the library that might hold clues to who killed Credence. You should come check it out." Nodding her head in punctuation, she pressed send.

"Thank you," Lou said.

"He's writing back." Willow's shoulders dropped as she read the message that came through moments later. "Busy with an actual case, Willow. Someone robbed the hardware store and I'm trying to track them down. Will look into your clues about a supposed crime when I have time." She wrinkled her nose, scowling down at her phone.

Lou's shoulders sagged forward.

"Well, that was rude," Willow scoffed. "You know, he had me all fooled the other day when he was being nice to OC, but this proves he hasn't changed one bit." She shook her head.

Lou let the disappointment settle over her—both about the detective's dismissal of their clues and of the step back he'd taken with Willow. Finally, she said, "I guess that means it's up to us to gather more evidence."

"Cool. Great. I'm in. It's just…" Willow wrinkled her nose. "I might not have a lot of free time until after the festival on Friday night. Once that's over, I'm all yours."

Lou understood. "That's okay. I've been closing the shop early lately, so I should keep it open during the full hours for the rest of the week. We can reconvene after the festival. Maybe we can even corner Easton during Spring Fling and see if he'll listen to us in person."

Willow grabbed her purse from inside her desk drawer. "Once we show him that secret room, he'll have to take us seriously."

Lou hoped that would be the case. There was still a murderer on the loose in town, and they needed to be brought to justice.

CHAPTER 18

The next day, Silas had just settled onto the couch with Catnip Everdeen, and Forrest was walking across the street with a coffee in hand when the bookshop's front door banged open. The bell jangled once in distress as it clattered, stuck between the door and the wall.

Lou frowned as she looked up. Owen stormed inside, a cat carrier at his side. All the shop cats bolted into hiding places. From the tautness of Owen's shoulders to the anger behind his eyes, Lou was momentarily worried he was going to slam the cat carrier down on the ground. But he set it down carefully and Lou exhaled her relief.

Silas stood, watching the man. The old man seemed to understand that even though Owen had been gentle with the cat, whatever he was about to say would not be.

"You didn't tell me this was Credence Crowley's cat." Owen's face was red. Spit flew from his mouth as he pointed at Lou and then at the cat carrier. His hands formed claws, then he pulled them into fists as he paced. "Trying to trick me into taking ... if you knew what that monster put me through ... there's no way!" He yelled sentence fragments as he paced.

Lou put a hand up to calm him. "Owen, I'm so sorry. I don't write the former owners on any of the cats, for privacy reasons." That was true, at least. "I didn't mean to upset you. You two just had such a connection."

He whipped around, staring her down. Anger flashed in his brown eyes, but Lou couldn't help but see the hurt there too. He flinched as his gaze landed on the crate. "I can't take anything that was his. I won't." He stormed out of the shop and disappeared down the street.

Forrest stood at the shop entrance, holding his cup of coffee, in shock. Silas shook his head, unfurled his newspaper, and sat back down on the couch.

"Sorry for the scene, everyone," Lou said, even though the only two customers to witness were her regulars. She moved around the register counter and knelt next to the crate. "Hi, Jules." The tabby cowered in the back of the crate, her pupils were large. "I'm sorry I put you in that situation," Lou whispered.

Making sure the front door was closed again, she opened the crate door and let Jules out, scooping her into a warm hug until she calmed. The cat relaxed in her arms and purred. Lou let her down as the other cats began venturing forward again after the loud noises.

Lou stood and met Forrest's concerned gaze.

"You did nothing wrong in that situation, Lou," Forrest said softly as if they were having a therapy session and she'd just confessed a fear of hers.

Lou shrugged. "I did, though. I knew it was Credence's cat, and I chose not to tell anyone because I knew it would affect the number of people who would be interested in her. I kept it from Owen when he adopted her." She watched the poor tabby. She was so sweet and deserved a loving home.

Forrest nodded. "Well, now you know that's something you might want to share with potential adopters," he said. "The right person won't care." He patted Lou on the shoulder and continued on to sit in the reading area with Silas.

Sighing, Lou knew he was right. Plus, the cat had only just gotten there. She wasn't in a rush to get rid of her.

THE REST of the day went by much less dramatically, thank goodness.

When Lou was about to close, Noah and his daughter, Marigold, came through the door. Marigold had a baseball mitt tucked under one arm, and her face was flushed from exercise. She must've been at practice for the fastpitch team Noah had mentioned.

"Just a few minutes, honey," Noah called to Marigold as she scampered off to the children's section, waving to Lou on her way by. "Lou's closing soon and we don't want to keep her."

Lou shook her head. "She's fine. I actually don't have any plans tonight, so I can stay open a little later if she wants to browse or play with the cats." Marigold's mother, Cassidy, was allergic, so she couldn't have a cat of her own. She got her fix by coming in and helping Lou pet and brush the cats in the bookstore at least once a week.

Noah's jaw clenched as he noticed the cat carrier still sitting on the floor. Lou had tucked it under the register counter so it wouldn't be in the way of customers, but it was still visible.

"Easton texted me earlier saying he'd made a huge mistake." Noah inhaled, sucking the breath through his teeth. "He saw Owen at the pet store getting cat toys and asked him when he'd adopted a cat. Owen explained, and Easton blurted out, 'Oh, Credence's cat. Right?' before he could think of the implications. He said Owen went crazy after that. Ranting and tossing cat toys all over the aisle. East feels awful about it and hoped Owen would've calmed down, but … it doesn't look like he did."

"He did not," Lou said. "He was pretty upset. Poor little Jules. She's such a sweetheart."

"She really is. Someone will give her a good home, I'm sure of it." He stuck his hands in his jeans pockets. "How's our patient doing?" Noah scanned the shop for Purrt.

"I'm keeping him upstairs for some quiet," Lou explained. "But he's doing much better. Especially now that he's over being a diva and deciding he didn't want to take the supplements he previously loved." She chuckled.

Noah did too. "It's what I love and hate about cats. They're so fickle. But it's that attitude that makes it feel so special when they decide to care about you. You know it means a lot because they seem to dislike so many things."

Lou agreed. "That's a good way to put it." She looked around at Marigold, who was saying hello to each cat, scratching behind their ears, and giving them each a kiss on top of their head. "So Easton's still entrenched in this robbery case?" she asked.

"Yep. Sounds like it." Noah nodded. "But when he texted earlier, he said they may have gotten a breakthrough."

"They must've if he had time to go to the pet store," she scoffed. "He made it seem like he was eating and sleeping this case. But now that I hear he's—wait." Lou stopped. "Why was he at the pet store?" Easton didn't have any animals.

Noah cleared his throat. "I don't think that's my place to say." He tried to look at Marigold, but Lou pinned him with an intense stare and he finally broke. "Okay, I suggested he get a few things for OC and Steve. If he feeds them treats and associates his side of the fence with good things, maybe they won't run away any time he tries to catch them."

Lou bit back a smile. "That's very nice of you to suggest."

"He's really trying," Noah said, and even though it was technically about the horse and goat, Lou caught the deeper meaning behind it.

"I can see that," Lou said.

Marigold came skipping over to join them. "Dad's going to be a king on Friday," she told Lou.

It was funny. The first time Lou had met Marigold, she'd been polite but very shy—as many nine-year-olds have the tendency to be. But now that they saw each other regularly, the girl told Lou just about everything on her mind. Sometimes she couldn't get her to stop talking.

"I've heard," Lou said. "Spring King, alongside your mom."

"Spring Queen." Marigold curtsied.

"Are you looking forward to the festival?" Lou asked.

Marigold's eyes went wide. "Yes. I'm going to win a cake at the cakewalk."

"Oh, what's your favorite kind?" Lou leaned forward with interest.

"Lemon. No, Chocolate." She chewed on her lip. "Maybe strawberry."

Lou and Noah laughed.

From the planning side of the festival, it had been mostly worry and stress up to now. But seeing the excitement through a child's eyes made Lou realize why Willow was working so hard. There were a lot of expectations surrounding the event.

"Okay, kiddo. Let's get out of Lou's hair. We've got a date with a pizza tonight since I don't have any food in the house." Noah ruffled his daughter's hair and pulled her to him in a fatherly hug.

Every time she hung out with Marigold, Lou missed her two nieces. While she was an only child, Ben had an older brother. He'd given them two amazing nieces. And even though Lou chatted with them weekly, she wished she lived closer. Well, she *was* closer. They lived in Montana, so Washington was better than New York, but still not a short trip. She knew the girls needed a connection with her even more after losing their uncle.

Noah must've misinterpreted Lou's nostalgic expression,

because he said, "You said you don't have plans. Would you like to join us?"

Marigold sucked in a deep breath. "Yes, Lou! Please, come have dinner with us. It'll be so much fun!"

"How can I say no to that invitation?" Lou laughed. "Sure. I'll have dinner with you two. Let me lock up."

The evening air was pleasant, with just a hint of chill moving through the quiet streets as the sun dipped lower in the sky. Lou and Marigold played the pinball machines in Slice of Button as they waited for their pizza. They won a pack of pink hair bows from the claw game and wore them throughout dinner, giggling whenever they caught their reflection in one of the pinball machine's glass fronts.

And even though it was nice to forget about Credence's death and his possible killer lurking out there, she knew the case couldn't wait forever. Spring Fling or not, someone out there had planned Credence's death to a T. Well, almost. They hadn't been perfect. There had been Jules, for one. And the button left on top of the pill container for another. The speck of lime-green glitter was also suspicious. One thing was for sure, the killer hadn't counted on Lou and her detail-oriented mind that made it almost impossible to look past things that didn't make sense.

As she lay in bed that night, Lou wondered if the killer had any idea she was onto them. For her safety, she really hoped they didn't.

CHAPTER 19

The next day, the sun was shining again. Purrt was on the mend and had rejoined the other cats, and Lou decided it would be the perfect evening to go on a nice long run.

She went on her usual route, heading west out toward Willow's house first. After the initial excitement of the beginning of a run, her breathing leveled out and came at a steady beat. Four counts in, three counts out.

And just as she always did, Lou slowed as she passed by the huge, overgrown mansion that sat on a piece of property in the middle of Thread Lane, Pin Street, and Pattern Drive.

The potted lily that had been there the other day was gone, replaced by a bright green succulent arrangement. Through a window on the front of the house, a shimmer of yellow light was visible inside.

Someone lived there; she was sure of it.

Lou and Ben had often chatted about their surroundings as they ran together. Sometimes it was a person or couple they saw all the time as they ran through Central Park. They loved to make up stories about their lives and why they were there each day.

They did the same about apartments they passed by or businesses they frequented.

So maybe she was doing the same thing here, needing a story to quell the curiosity running through her mind each time she passed by the mysterious mansion. But it also felt like something more. Like another puzzle she needed to solve.

Lou took a right up Pattern Drive and curved with the road as it came up by the middle and elementary schools. She ran down Stitch Street, loving the cute, colorful houses in that neighborhood.

One particular house stood out among the rest today. It was a small, green cottage that had about a dozen gnomes in an extensive front garden. Betsy, the former bus driver? Lou remembered Evelyn telling her about how her friend had gone a little gnome crazy in her retirement.

Without thinking too much about what she was doing, Lou jogged up the driveway and followed the stone steps that wound over to the front porch. She rang the doorbell and waited, breathing deep as she caught her breath.

It took a moment, but just as Lou was about to give up and go home, a woman opened the door. She looked a lot like Evelyn, actually, and Lou could see right away that they were friends. Their gray hair was styled in just about the same way, a long braid tossed over one shoulder. Reading glasses were perched on this woman's nose, just as Evelyn's had been the first day Lou had met her. They even dressed alike, khaki pants with a floral blouse.

"Hello?" Betsy frowned as she studied Lou, obviously not recognizing her.

"Hi," Lou said and smiled, hoping to create a more friendly picture. "I'm Louisa Henry. I bought the bookshop a few months ago." She held out her hand.

The woman took it but shook it warily. "Oh, that's nice." She was obviously unsure why Lou was here on her doorstep.

"I'm sorry to bother you. I've been working with your friend

Evelyn up at the high school library, and she mentioned you used to drive buses for the school district." Lou clasped her hands behind her back to keep herself from fidgeting. "You're Betsy, right?" she asked, just to make sure she wasn't at some other random gnome-lover's home.

The woman nodded. "That's me. Evelyn mentioned you were helping her with a big order. How lovely. How can I help you?" she asked.

"I'd love to talk with you about something. Is this an okay time?" Lou unclasped her hands, letting them swing free.

"Sure." Betsy motioned to two chairs set up on the front porch, overlooking her well-tended garden. "Would you like anything to drink?"

"No, thank you." Lou took a seat. "I promise I won't take up too much of your time. I just had a few questions about"—she wet her lips—"Credence Crowley."

Betsy's inviting expression tightened at the name. "Oh, goodness. That boy." She shook her head. "He was a handful, but I was sorry to hear he took his own life. That's not something I wish on anyone."

Scratching at her cheek, Lou said, "I've been hearing stories of how much he bullied people while he was in school." And after, Lou added, "Did you see any of that on the bus?"

She snorted, a surprising sound coming from such a sweet, older woman. "All the time." Her eyes narrowed. "He was smart about it, though. Never did anything he knew he could get caught for. Scared his victims enough that they never told on him. We knew it was happening, but we also knew his parents wouldn't care. Believe me, we tried to tell them his behavior was out of control in elementary school, but they wouldn't listen."

"What do you mean he never did anything he could get caught for?" Lou asked, leaning forward. "How did you know he was doing anything if the kids wouldn't tell on him?"

"You just get a feeling about these things, you know?" Betsy said. "Especially after a few years of having him on my route. I drove that boy around from kindergarten until he was almost seventeen and got his first car working. There were the little things. Like, I would often find sewing buttons all over the floor on the bus when I took it back to the bus barn. Sometimes it would be tiny balls of paper or paper clips, but a lot of buttons. We didn't have cameras on the buses back then like we did at the end of my career, so I couldn't look back at what I missed while I was watching the road."

The mention of buttons stuck in Lou's brain. There had been one small button on top of the pill bottle next to Credence's body, as if it were the last move in a decades-long game of chess.

"Sometimes I would see him slipping back down in between the seats in the rearview mirror, like he'd just popped up and tossed something at one of the other kids, but it was never enough to catch him. And when the kids wouldn't say anything, I could never get proof it was him." Betsy opened her hands, letting them fall into her lap.

"How about Flora Lucas?" Lou asked, using the principal's maiden name. "Was she on your route too?"

"Yup. Always knew that girl would make something of herself and look at her now. She's running that place." A proud smile pulled across Betsy's face.

Lou kept her questions about Flora's character to herself, seeing how much the woman was loved and respected in the community. She was like Credence's opposite in so many ways.

"I heard she was one of Credence's biggest targets." Lou watched the old bus driver, knowing visions of each of these kids growing up throughout the years were likely rushing through her memories.

Betsy's head dipped forward. "I mean, sure. He picked on her, but there weren't many kids stronger willed than that little Flora."

Lou listened, interested in this different take on the high school principal.

"She was so sure of herself, that little one," Betsy said. "And I saw many a red face covered in dried tears after riding with Credence, but never Flora's. She's made of strong stuff."

Lou contemplated this. As much as this fit with the strong, in-charge woman who led the school now, Lou couldn't help but wonder if it was all an act. Some people seemed strong and in control, yet they were using every fiber of their energy to keep up that appearance. Flora could've resented Credence for making her have to do that for so many years. That kind of resentment could last decades, even a lifetime.

"And there's no one else on that bus route you could think of that Credence bullied more than the others?" Lou asked.

Betsy shrugged. "Not especially. Sorry."

"That's okay," Lou said.

"Why are you asking about all of this, anyway?" Betsy asked. "Are you writing an article or something?"

"Something like that," Lou said absentmindedly. She stood and waved goodbye to Betsy. "Thank you for taking the time to talk to me."

"See you around, dear. I'll have to stop at the bookstore someday soon. Do you have any books on gardening?" Betsy stood and squinted in the sunlight.

"Tons!" Lou said, waving once more before turning to jog down the road.

Lou normally loved to listen to the sounds of her breathing, the birds chirping in the trees, the crunch of her shoes on the pavement. All of it was like a comforting soundtrack as she ran. But after what Betsy had told her, Lou's mind whirred with thoughts of Flora and Credence during the rest of her run home. Even dinner and her usual reading time in the evening were dominated by these thoughts and worries.

Because it just didn't add up.

Flora had been one of Credence's biggest targets, along with Owen. Lou sighed at the thought of Owen, but the reminder of the way he'd reacted when he learned whose cat Jules used to be showed how deeply Credence had damaged him, and how long internal scars lasted.

So even though she seemed to hide them better than Owen, Flora had to hold those same scars, if not more, right? Except Betsy was so sure she didn't.

But if Flora had nothing to do with what happened to Credence, why had she lied about her anniversary dinner? Then there had been the lime-green sparkle, just like on the card she'd kept on her desk. The secret room in the library, too, with the same writing as Flora's desk calendar.

Everything pointed to Flora, but it still felt like a puzzle piece that looked right but wouldn't quite fit into the correct place.

Before she went to bed, Lou texted Willow.

> Any luck talking to Easton?

Willow answered right back.

> He's been gone all evening. I think they were getting close to catching that robbery suspect. I'm not even sure if he'll be able to make it to the Spring Fling tomorrow, which means I'm going to be running the dunk booth by myself. Yay.

Lou responded that she would be there to help as well. She chewed on her lip as she put her phone on her bedside table and petted Sapphire, who was snuggled up in her lap in bed.

The other cats acted like they'd been tortured and ignored during the few days she'd kept Purrt up here by himself. They were practically drowning her with attention now that they were allowed back upstairs, but Lou didn't mind having multiple purring cats hanging around her.

As she drifted off to sleep that night, her mind ran through the clues, hoping something would fit. There was more at stake here than just a finished puzzle. This was about justice. And justice for a sour, angry person was justice all the same.

CHAPTER 20

Lou closed the bookshop early the next day so she could go up to the high school and help Willow with the Spring Fling set up. She felt okay about the decision even though it was Friday because, if the talk throughout the bookshop that day was any predictor, the whole town was going to be at the festival, anyway.

The high school parking lot was already crowded with cars, and Lou wondered whether they would be lined down the block once the festival was in full swing. Local people probably knew to walk, as she was doing, so they didn't have to worry about the traffic.

Lou chuckled at that thought. Traffic. The mild backup that would take place after the festival was nothing compared to rush hour in New York City. It was funny how quickly she was acclimating to small-town life after living in the big city for the last two decades.

The festival booths and activities were set up in the track-and-field area of campus, but Lou went inside first, knowing Willow had asked her to meet her there. When she arrived at the classroom, Lou initially thought she'd gotten lost and had walked into the wrong room.

Willow was nowhere to be found, and all the tables had been moved to the sides of the room. Checking the number on the outside of the classroom, Lou confirmed it was Willow's. She must already be out on the field getting ready. One would think getting outside to the field would be easy—all she needed to do was locate an exterior door. But Lou still got lost twice in the process.

Then before she even found one of the outside doors, she saw Easton walking toward her, tossing a softball up and down, probably for the dunk tank.

"Easton. Hey." She rushed over to him. "You catch your robbers?"

His eyes lit up as he came to a stop. "Sure did. You looking for Willow? She's out by the track," he said.

Checking the time, Lou realized she was a little earlier than she had said she'd be, which meant she had a few minutes to spare.

"Can I show you something?" she asked, grabbing his arm and pulling him in the direction of the school library—at least, she hoped it was the right direction.

Easton didn't dig in his heels and stop, but he did lean back in defiance as he followed her. "Wait. Does this have to do with the text I got from Willow the other night? Because I checked with Timothy, and he admitted to being tired and confused. He misspoke when he said he'd been driving the girls around to get them to fall asleep. He really was at poker with his friends. They all confirmed."

That was news to Lou. She appreciated the fact that Easton had looked into it even though he'd brushed off Willow via text.

"Thank you for asking about that," she said, aware she was going to seem very ungrateful with what she was about to say. "Did you ask Flora why she lied about her anniversary, though?"

Lou stopped in front of the library doors. The lights were off inside, showing Evelyn had already left for the day.

Easton shook his head. "Lou, I don't think you understand. Flora isn't ... there's no way she..." He frowned.

"I get it. She seems happy, but that's all on the outside. I think she's still holding a grudge all these years later." Lou opened the library doors and gestured inside. "Let me show you something that might change your mind."

Easton closed his eyes, fatigue evident in his posture, but he opened them and followed Lou inside.

"There's a secret room back here in the storeroom." Lou opened the storeroom door and flicked on the light.

"The building's full of defense shelters," Easton said, intrigue lifting his tone from the fed-up monotone he'd sported until now.

Lou moved to the side of the bookshelf snug against the wall and pushed with her shoulder until the large piece of furniture slid to the right. Easton gaped at the entrance even though she'd warned him about what they were going to see. Gesturing for Easton to follow her as she slid through the opening, she held her breath and groped around for the light switch, scared it would all be gone. What if the killer knew she was onto them and cleared out any evidence they'd forgotten back here?

But when Lou turned on the light, everything was still where she'd left it after showing Evelyn. The poster of the horse and the boy band were still stuck to the brick with gum. The pictures of cute boys and the one of Credence sat below those.

Easton glanced around. "Whoa. I never knew this place existed."

"I don't think many people did. Evelyn didn't even know, and she's been the librarian here for almost thirty years." Lou motioned for him to come closer to the wall.

She pointed to the picture of Credence, eyes having obviously been poked out by a tack or the point of a pen.

"Look. Whoever hung out in this place hated Credence. And

they had to have been here close to twenty years ago because of the poster." She gestured to the boy-band poster. "As well as the Tab and the Squeeze It." She gestured to the drink containers for brands she hadn't seen for decades.

Easton studied the list. "And they thought I was cute." His lips pulled into a boyish grin.

Lou snapped her fingers at him. "Focus. Evelyn said Flora was one of her teacher helpers. She would disappear back here for hours. This matches her handwriting too." Lou pulled out her phone and showed him the picture of Flora's desk calendar. "And here's the proof she lied to you about her anniversary."

"It doesn't look like this was just Flora," Easton said, brushing off the calendar picture. He pointed to the "we" written on each of the signs. "If it was *actually* Flora who hung these," he added, showing Lou he hadn't fully bought into Flora as the primary suspect.

"I've considered that," Lou admitted. "What about the possibility that she didn't act alone? What if two friends who were bullied by Credence made a pact, here in this secret room, to kill their bully twenty years later? You were in school at the same time as Flora. She obviously noticed you. Do you remember who she used to hang out with?"

Easton ran a hand through his hair. "I don't. Honestly, Flora and I didn't become friends until after we graduated. The most I can remember when we were in high school was seeing her clutching an armful of books, skittering off somewhere alone." He grimaced at how that sounded. "I just don't see someone holding a grudge that long."

"You did," Lou said, her voice quiet. She met Easton's eyes. "You still hated the guy for what he did to you twenty years ago."

Easton didn't get angry, as Lou feared he might at her statement. Instead, his expression softened. "Disliking a person for being mean is different from hating them enough to kill them, Lou. I'm sorry. But I'll see if I can talk to Flora about her anniversary, if that makes you feel better. She'll be here tonight. Okay?" Easton asked, trying to catch Lou's downcast eyes.

"Thank you," she said.

Easton checked his watch. "I'd better head out to the field. I wouldn't want Willow to think I chickened out or anything." He smiled.

Lou did, too, despite the letdown of Easton not seeing as much as she did in the clues. And maybe it was because they were in a secret room, but Lou felt emboldened to ask a question she might not have out in the open.

"You really care for her, don't you?" She held Easton's gaze.

Surprise wrote itself across his face, but he seemed to recognize that he wouldn't get away with any lies around an observant person like Lou.

"I do." Easton let out a humorless laugh. "Not that she'll ever see it that way. We're stuck in this antagonistic merry-go-round. She hates me."

Lou squinted. "I can't speak for her, but I think you might be wrong there."

Easton sighed. "I mean, it started out being real. I hated James. Hated him with a passion. Everyone else in town, including Willow, is so charmed by him. I felt like the only person who could see through his veneer."

"Willow isn't charmed by him anymore. She sees who he really is now." Lou watched him.

Easton cocked his head to one side. "I know. But once James left, I didn't know how to stop the hateful neighbor relationship we had going. I didn't want her to think I was trying to swoop in. She'd just gotten out of a long relationship, one that didn't end well. I knew she needed time to heal."

Lou's heart warmed at hearing Easton talk about her best friend like that, with the care she knew Willow deserved.

"You did pretty well the other day," she pointed out. "Caring about OC's cut and calling Noah to come check on him. You also didn't get mad at OC for eating your vegetables."

Easton ran a hand along his jawline. "I've always cared about that horse. It was just an easy thing to complain about to James, instead of what I really wanted to yell at him about, which was how a guy like him had landed a girl like Willow." Easton shrugged. "I couldn't care less if that silly horse eats a few of my vegetables." He glanced over his shoulder. "Actually, I think I might be the reason he gets into my garden. The first few times he was grazing when they moved in, I may have fed him a carrot or two over the fence."

Lou found his admission very sweet. "Keep showing her that side of you, Easton. You know she loves that horse more than life. I think she even likes him more than me."

Easton nodded. "I think you might be right."

"I can't promise she'll come around, but she deserves someone who cares for her like you seem to." Lou motioned toward the opening in the wall, noticing the time.

Easton followed. "Thanks. When you moved to town, I saw an opportunity to change how she saw me. I tried to help you as much as I could, thinking if you saw me as a nice guy that you could help change her mind."

Lou's heart melted. She'd noticed that Easton had dropped everything to help her during her first couple of months in town. Some of the local cops had even commented that he was doing too much for her. It all made sense now.

"As sweet as that is, you know there's no way anyone can change Willow's mind but Willow." Lou shot him a pointed look.

"I know." Easton held up his hands like she'd caught him red-handed.

"But I think you need to give her credit. She sees the things you do," Lou said.

"Thanks, Lou," he said. "Speaking of things we do for her"—

he tossed the softball into the air—"I'm going to go get plunged into cold water repeatedly for her."

Lou laughed. "See you around, Easton. When you see Willow, would you let her know that I'm waiting in her classroom?"

He gave Lou a salute.

Lou walked to Willow's classroom, thankful when she found her inside, flipping through copies of the festival schedule.

When she saw Lou, Willow waved her over. "Do you remember which version is the final one we decided on?"

Lou peered over her friend's shoulder. "That one." She pointed to the last one she changed the other day.

"That's what I thought." She nodded. "Okay, ready to set up?"

"Ready," Lou said. "Put me to work."

Lou watched her friend, thinking through what Easton had just told her, but she kept it to herself, knowing her best friend deserved to be won over; she deserved the world. Lou hoped Easton could be the person to give that to Willow.

Together, she and Willow carted out a load of supplies to the field, delivering schedules everywhere they went.

Through all the joyful festival setup, however, Lou couldn't help but feel like she was missing something big about Credence's death. The things she learned over the last two weeks only solidified the fact that the man hadn't taken his own life. And with the whole town here for the festival, his killer was likely here at the high school tonight.

CHAPTER 21

Between the festival setup and saying hello to the locals, Lou and Willow were hopping for the next hour. The Spring Fling had officially started, and Lou couldn't help but let a lightness fill her as she surveyed the people of Button at the high school track and field. It was a true celebration.

Someone had mowed the field for the event, and the sharp scent of cut grass surrounded her. Added to that were the sweet scents coming from the funnel-cake stand and the salty addition of the student-run popcorn booth.

Lou slowly let go of the urgency she felt earlier regarding Credence's death and finding his killer. This wasn't a situation where more lives were at stake. At least, she didn't believe it was. Credence had obviously been the target, and once he was gone, the killer would've been happy—theoretically. There wasn't a rush.

So she allowed herself to enjoy the festival. Lou stood in for Lindsey at the bakery booth so she could go run her donation over to the cakewalk. Lou ran errands for Willow, making trip after trip back to the classroom to grab lists or extra rounds of red tickets for the various booths.

It was good to feel helpful, especially since she saw how much it meant to her best friend for this to go well. Willow may have complained about the festival during the weeks leading up to it, and sworn she would never volunteer to lead it again, but today her posture was straight and the smile on her face wide. She was proud of what she'd accomplished.

Lou wouldn't be surprised if she said yes to chairing the event next year as well.

Without a job to do for a moment, Lou wandered through the festival activities and booths. The flower decorations were beautiful, green paper vines full of blooms linking one booth to the next. The students had added a few glittery flowers to each bunch.

Wandering by the Material Girls booth, Lou bought a few tickets for the quilt auction, wondering if Noah had helped with any of the sewing. She thought back to the first time she'd met him in his family's quilt shop, wearing that pink apron.

Lou waved as she saw Forrest walking through the festivities with his wife, Gianna, arm in arm.

"Hi, Lou," Forrest said. "Give Willow my compliments on the event. It's better than ever."

Lou nodded. "She'll be happy to hear that."

"And the weather's just beautiful," Gianna commented, looking around at the cloudless blue sky and evening sun shining down on them.

They chatted for a little longer until Forrest and Gianna wandered off again.

George waved from the line in front of the funnel-cake booth, but Lou saw she was with some of the Dungeons and Dragons group and didn't want to chance running into Owen, so she waved but didn't walk over.

Lou ran into Hannah and Sage next. The little girl ran over to Lou, exclaiming, "Miss Lou, Miss Lou! Catsby is doing great. Except we're calling him Beans now because he ate a bean off my plate the other day." She giggled.

"I'm so happy to hear that." Lou knelt down, so she was closer to Sage's height. "What's his favorite spot to nap in the house?"

Sage scrunched up her nose and giggled. "My bed. He loves my stuffed animals."

Hannah nodded. "He's one spoiled cat, that's for sure."

Lou was so relieved. It wasn't as if she didn't trust Hannah and Sage, but Beans had been kicked out of his last home for scratching and ruining furniture. There had been a slight worry in the back of her mind that he might start that up again.

"That's good. He deserves all the spoiling you can give him." Lou waved goodbye as the mother and daughter continued on toward the balloon station.

Moving into the field, Lou watched as another round of the cakewalk started. Marigold was taking part, a huge grin on her face as she went around the circle, jumping from number to number as the music played. She waved to her parents, who stood just outside the circle in the audience.

Lou walked over to Cassidy and Noah. Though she saw Noah a lot because of the cats, Lou had actually met Cassidy first—over video call. She'd been Lou's real estate agent and had helped her purchase the bookshop a few months prior.

The two were observing their daughter, laughing at her antics within the walk.

"Hey," Cassidy said as Lou walked over. "Everything looks great."

Lou nodded. "Willow and the kids worked really hard."

"I hear you helped a lot," Cassidy said.

"As much as I could." Lou frowned when she noticed Bea from the furniture store was calling the cakewalk. "I thought you two were running this."

"Marigold didn't want it to seem like we rigged it if she won, so we're sitting out this round." Noah rolled his eyes.

"Don't roll your eyes at that. She learned that sense of justice from you." Cassidy laughed.

Lou did too. She had definitely noticed the nine-year-old's intense sense of justice and empathy before.

At that moment, Marigold let out an excited squeal, jumping up and down as she won the cake in her round. She looked at her parents, wide-eyed, a smile sparkling.

Noah, Cassidy, and Lou all cheered for her, watching as she went over to choose a cake from the lineup on a table to the right. Marigold must've known going into the event which one she wanted, because she walked right up to an enormous chocolate cake—the very one Lou had seen Lindsey carrying over earlier—and pointed to it. Bea carefully extracted it from its place on the table and handed it over to Marigold. The thing was almost as big as the little girl, and the grown-ups laughed as she tottered away with it.

"We're going to take a brief break," Bea explained to the surrounding crowd. "The next cakewalk will happen in fifteen minutes. There's still time to buy your tickets. We have a couple of spots open in the next round."

Marigold reached her parents, holding out the cake like it was a crown jewel. "I won." She beamed.

"You did." Noah carefully took the cake from her, seeing the sheer weight of it was quickly becoming too much for her.

"Can we eat it now?" Marigold's eyes widened as she admired the chocolate dripping down the sides of the large cake.

Cassidy clicked her tongue. "Why don't we wait until we get home, sweetie?"

"But if we take it home, I won't be able to share it with anyone." Marigold pushed out her bottom lip in a pout.

Of course, the sweet child would want to share her prize. She had such a good heart. It wasn't about digging into the sweets herself; it was about sharing with others.

Noah looked down at his daughter with a proud smile. He turned to Cassidy, who pressed her lips together as she reconsidered the child's question.

"I wonder if there's a knife or plates in the teacher's lounge or office." Cassidy searched the crowd for someone who might help.

"I can go check," Lou said, wanting the parents to stay with Marigold. "I'm sure Willow would know. I'll be back in a minute."

"Thank you," Cassidy and Noah said in unison.

Noah put a hand on Marigold's shoulder. "While we wait for Lou to come back, what do you say we go dunk Easton a few times?"

Marigold's face lit up and Lou chuckled. Given the family's history on local softball and baseball teams, the detective was about to be in trouble.

Lou walked toward the high school building, trying to pre-plan her trip inside so she might not get lost on her way to the staff lounge. On her way past the funnel-cake stand, she noticed they had plates. She could always purchase a few from them if she couldn't find any inside. But with all of that batter, they wouldn't have the need for a knife.

Even with her plan, Lou still made her way down the hall and found she'd gone one floor up by accident. It took her a few turns to find her way back downstairs to the office, but she finally pulled open the office door and walked through the space toward the staff lounge.

As she passed by the desks of Mrs. Hovley, Mrs. Kyle, and Mr. Jennings, a lime-green sparkle caught her eye. She craned her neck to see a card propped on Mrs. Kyle's desk. It was the same handmade thank-you card Flora had on her desk. In fact, all of the office workers had the same cards. Lou remembered back to Willow mentioning the flowers were for administration appreciation month. Everyone in the office must've gotten a card from the kids. Narrowing her eyes as she thought, Lou passed all the way through the office and into the teacher's lounge.

The lounge held a few worn chairs along the wall and a large table in the center for teachers to eat lunch at, if they chose. It smelled like popcorn and whatever the teachers had heated for lunch that day.

Lou went straight for the drawers next to the old dishwasher and opened a few before she found a couple of old knives. There was a large serrated bread knife, a couple of small paring knives for fruit, and then one butcher's knife. Lou felt the butcher's knife would probably work best for the substantial cake, but it was so large that she worried she might scare people if she carried that into the festival.

Checking the next few drawers, Lou found a cake server. The edges were rounded, and it looked like a much safer option to bring into a festival. Next, she found a bag of plastic forks. She even found a small stack of paper plates. Grabbing a few napkins, she was about to leave when something on the counter drew her attention.

It was a plate of cookies. They had a tented sign next to them that read *No-bake Peanut Butter Cookies. Enjoy.*

Blue cellophane covered the plate.

Just like the plate Liza had mentioned seeing on Credence's doorstep the night he died. Even more, without even having it next to her, Lou could tell right away that the handwriting matched that of the yearbook back at her apartment.

Easton had said there had been peanut butter cookies in Credence's gut. And no-bake cookies would be a perfect way to get drugs into someone, since Easton mentioned baking them could affect the potency of the drug.

Lou set down the plates and utensils, her hands shaking as she brought out her phone and dialed Willow's number. It rang four times, and Lou was worried she wouldn't pick up.

"Hey, what's up?" Willow answered at the last second. "I haven't seen you for a while. Where are you at?" The sound of crowds in the background made it hard for Lou to hear her.

"In the staff lounge, grabbing utensils. Willow, who made the cookies that are in here?" she asked.

"Oh, there are some left? You should totally have one. They're to die for. Mary makes them, if you can believe it. I think it's another reason people put up with her poor attitude. She bakes super yummy things for the staff weekly. In fact, would you grab an extra for me while you're in there?" Willow chatted, not realizing anything was wrong.

Another reason people put up with her poor attitude. Lou remembered back to the first reason Willow had given as to why the staff supposed Mary had kept her job all these years: she'd been Flora's neighbor, growing up.

Lou's throat constricted, making it hard to breathe. She swallowed. "Mary?" she asked in a whisper.

Then it all came crashing down on her.

What if Flora and Mary were more than just neighbors? What if they'd been friends? They would've been on the same bus route, along with Credence.

If Mary and Flora were friends, they could've found the secret room together. Had they worked together to take care of their old bully all these years later?

The chatter on Willow's end increased like she'd just walked up to a crowded booth. The reminder of the festival brought the reason Willow was running the event to mind. Mary was usually the one who oversaw the event, but she'd said she had other things going on this year. What if one of those things was executing a decades-long plan to murder her childhood tormentor and pass it off as suicide?

"Willow, I need you to find Easton. It's important. I think Mary is the one who killed Credence." Lou's voice cracked as she willed her friend to hear her over the noise of the festival. "Flora might have helped her," Lou mumbled, more to herself than Willow.

"What?" Willow asked, loud cheers erupted in the background. "Sorry, I couldn't hear that last part. Marigold just rocketed a ball straight at the bull's-eye on the dunk tank and Easton went in." Willow laughed.

"Mary. I think Mary might've killed Credence," Lou repeated, louder this time. "Tell Easton I'm coming to find him."

"Easton?" Willow said as if that was the only part she could hear. "He's just climbing out of the dunk tank, but I'll let him know you're searching for him. Okay, I've gotta go."

Willow hung up the call. It had been too loud, and she must've missed the tension in Lou's voice.

Lou glanced down at the plate of cookies and then at the stack of cutlery she was bringing outside. She needed proof if she had any chance of convincing Easton. Lou placed the cookies and the sign onto the stack and brought them with her as she left the teacher's lounge.

But as she sped into the main office, she found she wasn't alone anymore. A chill wound down Lou's spine as her gaze landed on someone else in the office. Mary Hovley stood next to her desk, fixing Lou with a terrible glare.

CHAPTER 22

Lou's breath left her body in a ragged exhale. Fear clutched at her throat.

How long had Mary been here? Had she heard Lou on the phone with Willow? Lou couldn't believe how silly she'd been to vocalize her suspicions over the phone without checking to see if she was still alone in the office.

Mary dropped the lipstick she'd been reapplying back into her handbag.

The woman's expression had darkened as she recognized Lou, but it turned flat out lethal when she noticed the cookies clutched in Lou's hands.

"What are you doing with those?" Mary snapped, her tone so sharp that Lou flinched at the sound.

Lou swallowed and took a step back. "These cookies?" she asked, trying to buy herself some time. There was no other way out of the room but through the office. "They looked so delicious that I thought I would bring them outside." Lou stumbled through the idea as it came to her.

Mary's jaw tightened with annoyance.

"To share," Lou added quickly. "With the people working at

the festival. I wanted to give them a pick-me-up in the form of a cookie." Her whole body was hot with worry, and she could feel sweat gathering on the back of her neck.

Don't say you know she made them. Don't say you know she made them, Lou repeated in her mind, knowing that admitting she knew Mary had made them would mean she'd asked around.

"And why do you have plates and forks?" Mary asked, placing a hand on her hip as if her tone didn't already scream, I don't believe you.

"Oh, that's for cake … from the cakewalk." Lou clutched the plates tighter so Mary might not notice her shaking fingers. Lou didn't want to describe too much. The more she said, the more of a chance she had of saying something she shouldn't in front of Mary.

Lou studied the woman, trying to discern if she was angrier than usual because she'd overheard that Lou knew what she'd done to Credence, or if this was just her normal level of anger and spite. Taking a chance that it was the latter option, Lou slowly walked toward the office door. As much as she wanted to move sideways, to keep Mary in her sights, Lou knew that would be suspicious. So she walked normally toward the door.

She tried to think through the facts as she walked. If Mary really had poisoned Credence, it made her a killer but a calculating one. She hadn't shot or stabbed or strangled him. Plus, Mary thought she'd gotten away with it. Lou didn't need to fear her.

Her fingers had just clasped around the handle when Mary's voice stopped her.

"Wait," the woman called out.

Lou closed her eyes for a split second, then opened them and turned around. She didn't trust her voice, so she didn't speak but lifted her eyebrows in question.

Mary stalked toward her. Yes, that was the motion. Stalking, like Lou was prey and Mary was coming in for the kill. Maybe Lou had been wrong about not needing to fear her.

Lou resisted every urge to close her eyes as Mary closed in on her. In her mind, she ran through terrifying scenarios of what she might do if Mary tried to hurt her. The woman couldn't be much over five feet tall, so Lou—who rarely felt tall—had a few inches on her. But she exuded a terrifying anger that told Lou she might snap at any second.

Mary met Lou's nervous, flickering gaze and held it for longer than was comfortable in a normal situation, let alone this stressful one. Mary's eyes narrowed, one twitched.

Does she know I know? Lou thought, feeling as if the question was written all over her.

Then Mary reached forward, flipped back the blue cellophane, and grabbed a cookie.

"One for the road." Mary took a bite and then backed away.

Lou let out a nervous laugh, way too loud. "Right." She turned and slipped out of the office door.

Would Mary come after her? Lou didn't wait to find out. She walked away from the office as quickly as she could.

The hallway outside of the office was deadly silent, reminding Lou that she and Mary might very well be the only two people inside the high school building at that moment. Everyone else was out at the festival, close but not close enough to hear Lou yell for help.

The realization made her quicken her pace. She took a right and then a quick left. The squeak of her sneakers against the linoleum floors echoed through the empty halls, making the hair on the backs of her arms stand up. Another squeak sounded, but this time from behind her.

Lou froze, heart pounding. Mary was following her.

Unable to hear as well as she wanted because her pulse beat so loudly in her ears, Lou picked up the pace and rounded the next corner. In her haste to escape, she'd arrived at a part of the building she didn't recognize.

She was lost.

Lou pulled in a shuddering breath. *Why now?*

That was when she heard footsteps again. A single squeak came from behind Lou, like the person was trying to be quiet, but the sole of their shoe had accidentally dragged along the floor.

Lou took in her surroundings. All the posters on the walls seemed to be English and literature themed. She'd never been down the humanities hallway. The windows to the outside were in the classrooms, so the hallway was just interior walls, and Lou didn't even know whether she was nearer to the front of the building or the back.

She saw a staircase in front of her that led down to the next level, the basement, but a chill rushed through her at the thought. No, she needed to find a way out, not down into a scarier section.

Peering around the corner, Lou found an empty hallway. She took a left this time. Maybe she could retrace her steps and get back to the main corridor. Another sound came from behind her, making the hairs on the back of her neck stand on end. Had that been a door closing? It had definitely been closer than the last sound.

The plastic forks and cake server she held would not help her against a murderer, and Lou wished she'd just grabbed the big knife. At least she would've had some protection.

Weaponless, Lou raced forward, taking the first right she could. Now her ears were really messing with her because Lou could swear she heard someone else breathing right over her shoulder.

The sensation pushed her forward faster, and she considered dropping the plates and cookies so she could use her arms and flat-out run. But she couldn't leave the cookies. They might hold a clue that Easton would need.

She rounded the next corner, running straight into a person.

Lou screamed. She threw the cookies and plates into the air and stumbled back.

But just as quickly as the encounter had happened, Lou recognized that the figure she'd run into was tall, not short, like Mary.

"Lou, what's going on?" Easton said, appraising the scattered plates, forks, and cookies. His hair was wet, but he'd obviously just changed into dry clothes.

Lou's entire body relaxed for a moment.

She wanted to sink to the floor in relief but knew she still had work to do.

"Easton, it's Mary. She did it. She killed Credence." Lou pointed to the cookies strewn around the floor. "She made those. See the blue cellophane. They're not baked so they wouldn't mess with the sleeping pills."

Easton blinked for a moment, like he was stuck buffering from a slow internet connection. "Wait. What? Mary?"

"It's her, she did it. She rode his bus, and he flicked buttons at Mary and Flora on the bus. That's why there was one button on the pill container. There was a spec of lime-green glitter on him, just like the card on Mary's desk. I think Mary hung out in the secret room in the library with Flora." She pulled in a breath after blurting all of that out.

"Mary and Flora were friends?" Easton asked, his gaze rising to study the ceiling

Lou nodded. "The only thing I'm not sure of is whether she had help." She knelt, picking up the cookies and plates.

"Who had help with what?" Flora asked, stepping into the hallway.

Lou resisted screaming again but moved closer to Easton. Surely Flora wouldn't hurt a police officer, right? Lou gulped, trying not to think too hard about it.

"I heard a racket and thought some kids had snuck inside during the festival." Flora folded her arms in front of her, staring at Easton like she still wasn't sure that's not what was happening.

Easton's expression hadn't changed through Lou's explanation, so she couldn't tell if he was buying any of it.

But he must've had at least a little doubt, because he said, "Flor, what were you really doing two Fridays ago?" Easton's tone was steady even though Lou's hands would've been shaking if she hadn't been holding on to the cookies. "I know it wasn't your anniversary."

Flora scoffed, "It absolutely *was* my anniversary."

"Then why does it say that your anniversary is April the seventh on the calendar in your office?" Lou's voice was small but steady. She counted that as a win.

Flora's face softened. "My wedding anniversary is in April. Kevin and I celebrate our dating anniversary as well, which was two Fridays ago."

Easton groaned. "You're *those* kinds of people."

Flora's mannerism softened immediately. She and Easton shared a teasing smile. These two were old friends, comfortable with each other.

"You can ask Kevin yourself. And the dozen other people we had dinner with at the bistro, if you'd like." Flora's stern-principal disposition was back. "Why do you care what I was doing that Friday night?"

Easton inhaled. He paused long enough that Lou knew he didn't want to say anything about Credence, still not quite convinced she was right.

"It's *possible* Credence didn't die by suicide. He *might've* been killed." Easton put so much emphasis on "possible" and "might've" that there was no way Flora could've gotten the wrong idea.

But Flora acted like she hadn't heard those words at all. Her skin tone paled, and she sucked in a gasp.

"No. It was just…" She petered out but shook her head.

"What?" Easton asked, frowning as he watched his old friend react.

"She knows it was Mary," Lou said. "I think they used to talk about Credence's death when they would hide out in the secret room in the library. You don't poke the eyes out of someone's picture if you don't wish them harm, after all." Lou watched Flora turn even paler as her eyes met Lou's.

"The secret room. I'd forgotten about that place." Flora turned to Easton. "We only ever joked about it—about how Credence would probably off himself—to make Mary feel better after he would torment her. He would flick buttons at her on the bus."

Lou's eyes widened at that statement. "He only flicked buttons at her? Not you?" Lou asked, thinking back to what Betsy had said.

Flora shook her head. "Mostly at her. Mary's prized possession when we were in elementary school was her button collection. She brought it one day for show-and-tell, but Credence stole it before she even got to school. He kept that bag of buttons for years. Those were the ones he flicked at her, repeatedly. He even called her Ugly Button. Mary was his target. He only ever picked on me because I stood up for Mary."

"So that was why she left the button," Lou muttered. "Mary won the last laugh at his expense."

Easton gestured toward Flora. "She just said they joked about wanting Credence to off himself, not about Mary doing the killing."

At this, Flora's gaze dropped to the floor. She grimaced.

"Right, Flor?" Easton asked.

"Why did the two of you stop hanging out?" Lou asked. When Flora didn't answer, Lou added, "Was it when she started growing bitter? Or did she talk about actually hurting Credence and it went too far for you?"

"It was after he stole her yearbook. She totally lost it. He grabbed it from her on the bus the day we got them, and Credence wrote in it before Mary could get anyone else to sign it," Flora explained. "She was so embarrassed that someone might read the awful thing he wrote, that she pretended she didn't buy a yearbook that year." The words tumbled out of Flora like a faucet that had been stuck but now was flowing just fine. "And after that, she started talking about how he would pay, how she would make him regret how he'd treated her. She became obsessed. That's when we stopped hanging out. It wasn't fun hanging out with her, because it's all she talked about. But I didn't think she was actually serious about any of it."

"I think she was," Lou said. "She planned everything to a T. Except that she couldn't help but leave a button at the scene."

Easton's mouth hung open slightly in shock.

"She made him cookies with a sleeping pill or two inside," Lou said. "Whatever was in the cookies must have been enough to get him to pass out so she could shove the rest of the bottle he had into him."

"How would she know he took sleeping pills?" Easton asked.

Shrugging, Lou said, "Maybe she overheard him at the pharmacy counter, or spied on him. I don't know. But what matters is she's the one who left the cookies on his doorstep." Lou gestured to the blue cellophane. "That's what Liza saw when she was sneaking around the property. Credence was too dense to understand that he probably shouldn't trust the cookies. Mary counted on that."

Flora nodded, proving it all checked out.

"The lime-green sparkle must've been on her hand or sleeve. They all got cards for office administration appreciation month." Lou looked at Flora. "Sorry, that's why I thought it was you for a moment."

"Me?" Flora whispered, blinking as she came to terms with the reality that she'd been a suspect in a murder investigation.

"But what about the suicide note?" Easton asked, scowling. "That was in his handwriting. We confirmed it. I doubt Mary could've convinced him to write any of that if he didn't want to."

Flora's hand flew up to cover a gasp. "She did Credence's

homework for most of high school. Believe me, if she hadn't the bullying would've been even worse. She was exceptional at faking his handwriting," she said.

That bit of information seemed to be the missing piece of the puzzle. Once he heard it, it was as if Easton finally could see the possibility of Mary as the killer. "Where is she right now?" he asked.

Lou glanced over her shoulder. "I saw her in the office, but I ran. I don't know if she heard me talking to Willow on the phone, telling her that I suspected it was Mary who killed Credence."

"Okay," Easton said. "I'll check there first, but she's probably already left the building and is on the run. You two head out to the festival where everyone else is. Call me if you see her." He waited for them to nod before jogging toward the office.

Lou stood awkwardly next to Flora for a moment as they watched Easton go. Once he was out of sight, they walked toward the festival.

"Sorry, I thought it was you," Lou said, eyes downcast as they walked. "For what it's worth, it never fully made sense. And no one who knew you would believe it. I should've trusted them. I just know that people aren't as happy and put together as they sometimes seem." Lou raised her hand. "Myself included."

Flora gave Lou a sympathetic head tilt. "Willow told me about your husband."

Lou turned to Flora in surprise, but then remembered that Willow had flown out to see Lou when Ben had died last year, so she would've shared the reason she needed to leave with her boss.

"I'm so sorry. I can't imagine," Flora said. And Lou knew she couldn't. It sounded like she and Kevin were just as in love and annoying as Lou and Ben had been. "I just can't believe Mary would do this." Flora squeezed her eyes shut. "I feel responsible."

"You shouldn't," Lou said.

"I've always felt bad about how we drifted apart as we got older." Flora shook her head. "It's partly why I hired her for the job here in the office once I got the principalship, and didn't fire her for being so sour all the time," Flora added, when Lou shot her a knowing look.

Willow and the other staff members had been right about that, it seemed.

They passed by the library, and Lou frowned as she thought about the footsteps she'd heard behind when she was running before. She'd assumed Mary was running after her.

But what if Mary hadn't been following her? What if she'd been running somewhere else? Somewhere no one else would think to look?

Lou halted, holding out a hand to stop Flora too. "I think Easton's searching in the wrong place."

CHAPTER 23

Flora's eyes locked on to Lou's as they both turned toward the library. Flora may have forgotten all about their hideout, but Lou would bet Mary hadn't.

"The secret room," Flora whispered. She chewed on her lip for a second and then looked to Lou. "You should go get Easton. I'll go try to talk her into turning herself in."

"That's too dangerous," Lou said.

"She was my best friend for most of our childhood. She won't hurt me." Flora attempted a smile, but it was more of a cringe.

Lou inhaled. "I don't think she'll hurt you, either, but I can't let you go by yourself. I'll go with you, and we can call Easton together if she's in there."

Flora agreed, and they stepped forward together.

The library was dark and quiet as they entered. Even with the lights off, the skylights above provided enough light that they weren't worried about running into tables or carts full of books. The storage room light was off as well, and Lou wondered if she'd made a mistake for a moment, but then a scraping sound came from the easternmost wall, from the direction of the secret room.

Tiptoeing into the back room, the two women found the bookshelf pushed aside. Light spilled out from the opening in the wall, confirming someone was inside.

"Mary," Flora called warily, glancing at Lou before she slipped through the opening. "It's me," she said.

Lou followed behind, and they stood there, taking in the sight.

The posters had been ripped from the wall as well as the list of cute boys. Credence's defaced class picture wasn't anywhere to be found either. Mary sat in the middle of a pile of yearbooks, flipping through the pages. Her bun was askew, and some of her hair fell forward into her face. She was muttering to herself.

"Mary," Flora said again, taking a step forward.

That was when Mary reached over, and on the floor next to her, she picked up a large knife. Lou recognized it as the same scary knife she'd been too reluctant to grab in the staff lounge kitchen. For the second time, she wished she'd just taken it.

Jabbing the knife in front of her in warning, Mary finally looked up. "Don't come any closer," she hissed, her eyes flicking from Flora to Lou. Then she went back to flipping through the yearbooks. "It's got to be here," she murmured, eyes wild as she searched the pages.

"Your yearbook? The one Credence wrote in?" Flora asked.

Mary's hate-filled eyes peered up to meet Flora's.

"It won't be in that pile," Lou said carefully.

"You took it?" Mary growled out the question.

She stood and jabbed the knife forward, causing Lou and Flora to jump to their right. Mary took the opportunity to step in front of the opening in the wall, blocking the only exit.

Lou put up her hands. "The yearbook wasn't in here. Your parents must've donated it, because it ended up at a charity shop. It came back to the high school in a donation of books."

Mary's expression dropped. "From Carol Joyce." Understanding dawned on her. "I knew you were up to something." Mary poked the knife toward Lou.

"It's going to be okay. Let's walk out there together and

explain what happened. I'll be right by your side." Flora put her hands up as she took in her old friend and the knife she was currently pointing at them.

"Of course it's not going to be okay." Mary shook her head. "I'm sure this one already told Easton everything."

Lou flinched. She had, and she wasn't sure if that fact helped her or hurt her at that moment. She decided it helped, if not only because Mary knew she couldn't kill both of them and think her secret would die with them. Before, she hadn't been worried about Mary being violent, but it was undeniable seeing her wield that large knife.

"Easton knows everything," Lou finally admitted.

Mary paced by the entrance. "Okay, let's see," she said to herself. Her mind must've latched on to an idea because she nodded and smiled. "Maybe that will work."

Her wild eyes latched on to a large roll of packing tape sitting on one of the bookshelves. Lou had seen Evelyn using a similar roll the other day to protect the covers and spines of library books before they went into circulation. Mary grabbed the tape and motioned with the knife. "Come here, both of you."

Flora and Lou glanced at each other questioningly.

Mary sighed. "You're going to tape Flora's hands behind her back. I'm going to watch. If you think of doing anything funny, I'll be right here to make you pay." She stepped closer, swinging the knife at Lou.

Lou gulped and looked at Flora apologetically but held out her hands for the tape, not sure if there was an alternative here. Trying to predict where she was going with the idea, Lou guessed Mary was going to tie them up in here and run. That didn't sound so bad. Flora shot Lou a hopeful look before turning around, proving she was thinking the same thing.

"Hands behind you, Flor," Mary said.

The ripping sound of tape being unrolled filled the small room as Lou started the tape, wrapping it around Flora's wrists.

"Two more times and we should be good," Mary said.

Lou wrapped the tape around Flora's wrists twice more. Ripping the tape with her teeth. Lou felt her phone buzz in her pocket. She wondered if it was Easton, but didn't dare reach for it with Mary standing within striking distance with the knife.

"Do her ankles too," Mary said, gesturing for Flora to sit on one of the mats."

Lou did as she asked.

"Okay," Mary said, nodding. "Turn around. Hands behind your back."

The thought of knocking over Mary and running crossed Lou's mind. She was fast. She could probably outrun her. But running meant she was leaving Flora in here with a knife-wielding killer. And even though Mary seemed averse to hurting her friend, Lou couldn't be sure what Mary was capable of, especially if pushed to the limit. Once Mary tied them both up and left, they could figure out what to do next without the threat of a knife in their faces.

Lou's hands shook as she complied, putting them behind her back. The tape bit into her skin and she realized Mary was making her bonds a lot tighter than Lou had with Flora's. Once Lou's hands were tied, and Mary ripped the tape, Lou moved to sit next to Flora on the mat, preparing to have her ankles taped too.

"No," Mary said, motioning with the knife. "You're coming with me." She pointed at Lou.

Lou's mouth dropped open.

"Wait. Where are you taking Lou?" Flora begged.

Mary rolled her eyes. "Well, I need a hostage to take outside with me, to help with negotiations. And even though I should hate you, Flora, I don't want to have to kill you, so you're going to stay in here where I'm sure you won't cause me any trouble."

Lou swallowed, and Flora's eyes met hers, full of fear.

"Let's go. No trying anything." Mary poked Lou's back with the edge of the knife to remind her of what she held.

As if Lou could've forgotten.

Lou walked forward, at least happy knowing that Flora would be safe where she was in the secret room. As for her own safety? She wasn't so sure about that.

Her heart hammered in her throat as she tried to imagine what would happen next. Lou couldn't see how taking any hostages could help Mary at this point.

"Where are we going?" Lou asked as Mary pushed her through the exterior doors of the high school and turned toward the field. "You know all the people are out here for the Spring Fling festival, right?"

"Exactly." The one word sent chills down Lou's spine, and she hoped Mary had a plan that involved something other than her stabbing Lou through the back in front of the whole town. "You're my ticket to a lighter sentence. If I can get Easton to make me a promise in front of all these people, he can't go back on it."

Lou frowned. She was almost positive that wasn't how hostage negotiations worked. Fear gripped her, and Lou considered kicking her and running, now that they were far enough away from Flora. But with her arms tied behind her back, she couldn't be sure Mary wouldn't catch up to her and stab her for trying to escape. The chance that this would all work out okay, that Easton would negotiate with Mary for Lou's life, was her best bet.

The festival looked just as it had when Lou had left for the plates and cake-cutting supplies. People laughed; a large crowd gathered around the dunk tank as someone else Lou didn't recognize had taken over for Easton.

Speaking of Easton, he must've been searching through the crowd because he caught sight of Lou and Mary walking forward and froze, standing on the edge of the track. At first, relief passed over his face like he thought Lou had merely convinced Mary to come outside with her and turn herself in. But his eyes flicked down to how she was holding her hands behind her back, and his posture stiffened as his concern grew.

"Easton, I need to speak with you." Mary pulled the knife away from Lou's back for a second to show the detective.

Someone in the crowd screamed as they noticed, and Mary pushed the tip into Lou's back once more as silence fell over the festival and people crowded forward.

"Don't get too close, or this is going to get ugly," Mary warned the people edging closer to Lou's left.

"Mary, what are you doing?" Easton asked, his tone thick as a block of ice. He stepped in front of the locals, holding his arms out to signal for them to stay back.

"I need you to promise me you'll give me a low sentence," she yelled, her voice sounding wild and crazed, like it had become entangled in the wind and swept away. "Promise me or I'll hurt her."

Easton adopted a pained expression as he walked forward one step. "That's not how it works, Mary." His voice was soft.

The tip of the knife dug into Lou's back a little farther. She winced.

Easton held up a hand but didn't move forward anymore. "But we can talk. Turning yourself in would give you the best chance." He grimaced. "Please don't hurt anyone else."

"I did us all a favor!" Mary yelled. Her fingers dug into Lou's arm as she added, "He was awful to everyone. He cheated people out of money. He made our lives miserable. Everything would've been fine if Miss Crime Solver here hadn't figured it out." She pointed the knife at Easton. "I even fooled you."

In the split second after she said that, something went flying in front of Lou's face. She flinched, but whatever it was had already flown past, hitting the knife Mary held, straight on. She cried out in shock, and her grip released as the knife was knocked from her hand.

It felt like it all happened in slow motion, but things sped up considerably after that. Easton yelled for Lou to get down, and he came barreling toward her as she felt Mary push her forward and make a run for it. The way she hit the ground knocked all the air out of her lungs, and Lou coughed, gasping for a moment before she could breathe again.

Someone pulled her up, and she saw Willow's face in her fuzzy vision.

"Lou? Are you okay?" Willow disappeared behind her, and she felt the tape being ripped from her wrists. Willow checked her back, where the knife had been pressed and sighed in relief. "She didn't cut her," she said to the surrounding crowd.

Lou rubbed at her wrists, scanning the crowd. Someone must've called the police because backup officers were there, assisting Easton with Mary, putting her in handcuffs. Then she glanced at the ground where the knife still lay in the grass. About a yard away, was a softball, the same kind they were throwing for the dunk tank. Lou's eyes flicked up to where Noah stood next to Cassidy, her eyes narrowed in question.

Both Cassidy and Noah shook their heads. But Cassidy's eyes practically sparkled as she looked down at her daughter. Noah wrapped an arm around Marigold's shoulders.

"Did I mention we taught her everything we know?" Noah said.

"Except that it was a very dangerous idea," Easton said, stepping forward. But his stern expression broke, and he smiled. "That probably saved Lou's life."

Marigold broke into a huge grin. So did Lou. She held her arms open and walked forward. Marigold met her halfway, tucking herself into Lou's arms.

"Thank you," she said into the girl's dark curls. Then she let out the kind of laugh that only comes after fatigue, exhaustion, and relief. She met Cassidy's and Noah's eyes. "You have quite the girl here."

Noah's dimples deepened. "We sure do."

Willow caught Lou's attention and leveled her with a serious stare. "Are you sure you're okay?" she asked, then added, "Honest three."

Lou pulled in a breath. "Shaky, surprised, grateful." She held Willow's gaze in an attempt to show her friend she was really okay. Suddenly Lou turned toward Easton, her eyes widening. "Flora! She's tied up in the secret room in the library."

"Secret room?" Marigold said, excitement leaking from her tone.

Noah shook his head in a *not right now* gesture, but Lou noticed he and a few others in the dispersing crowd looked interested at the mention of a secret room.

Easton waved to Lou. "Want to come with me to get her? I think she'll appreciate seeing you're okay."

Lou followed him toward the building.

"How'd she find out what you knew?" he asked once they were away from the crowd.

"She must've heard me on the phone with Willow." Lou regretted not checking to make sure she'd been alone. "Then she raced to the secret room to get rid of the evidence. Flora and I figured out that was where she'd gone once you left to go look for her. We didn't think she would be dangerous." A shiver ran down her spine at the memory.

Easton sighed as they entered the building. "None of us did. Boy, were we wrong. I'm so sorry. I should've taken you more seriously. Those details you noticed, they all turned out to be important." He shook his head. "I promise I won't discount your insight on cases anymore."

Lou scoffed, "Oh, believe me, I'm hoping this is my last murder investigation for a *long* while."

CHAPTER 24

The Sunday morning sunshine streamed through the front windows of Whiskers and Words, filtered through the bright green leaves of the ash-leaf maples Willow had put in front of the shop.

Lou absentmindedly rubbed at her wrists. There were no bruises, but they still ached from the tight tape Mary had used to bind them.

Lou had kept the bookshop closed yesterday, something which no one in town blamed her for, one bit. They'd all expected her to need more than a day to recover—and possibly start seeing Forrest to talk through her feelings about being held at knifepoint by a murderer.

But it had been weird without the shop open yesterday. She'd missed her quiet routines and her space behind the counter, playing with the cats as they hung out in the shop. She missed reading a book when the store was slow and people-watching as shoppers walked by on the busy streets of Button.

She'd spent the day with Willow on the farm. Helping her with barn chores had been a great way to keep her mind off what had happened yesterday. Between the beautiful horse and the adorable goat, Steve, Lou had been charmed and in stitches half the day. The company of her best friend didn't hurt either. Willow always knew just how to make Lou feel better. And she understood that having a job to work on while they talked was the perfect way for Lou to process what she'd gone through. It didn't hurt that she'd gotten to dress Steve in his pajamas and he'd spent the day looking too adorable for words.

Easton had even stopped by later in the evening to fill them in on Mary's status. After her public confession, they had transported her to the county sheriff's station in Kirk.

Easton had raised his hands and said, "She's in their hands now."

From the relieved expression on his face, it felt like a good thing. Lou imagined it had to be hard to arrest and book someone you'd grown up with.

Lou had gotten a text from George that night when she'd come home from Willow's.

We just wanted to check if you're going to be open tomorrow. Totally understand if not. The D and D group can meet at the library.

I'll be open. Come on over.

Lou had really enjoyed having them around last week.

But one question remained about the Dungeons and Dragons club as Lou set up the folding table for them in the back by the used-book section: Owen. Would he show up? He'd been so furious with Lou last time she'd seen him. Had his anger dissipated or grown in the days since he'd returned Jules? She wasn't sure how attached to the group he was, but it felt like something he might skip if they insisted on keeping it at the bookshop.

The club filtered in an hour later, answering her question. Owen was there. He did not, however, make eye contact with Lou, keeping his head down as they walked through and set up on the table. George and the others stopped to say hello before setting up.

The sound of unfamiliar voices and the clicking noise of dice being rolled invariably attracted the attention of the cats.

Purrt wandered over first, sniffing at the visitors' shoes and curling up on the floor near them as if he were supervising their game. Anne Mice tried to jump onto the table three times before Lou went to get her, taking her over to one of the cat beds near the front of the shop to nap instead.

But it was Jules's approach about half an hour into their game that made everyone at the table stop.

George swallowed and looked at Owen as Jules directed her love and affection toward him. "She's back," George said weakly, a smile trying at the corners of her mouth.

Owen had either told the group about his momentary adoption of her, or he was operating under no false pretenses about the rumor mill in the small town, because he assumed they knew.

"Doesn't mean anything." He sniffed, ignoring the tabby as she rubbed against his leg and stared up at him adoringly.

"Let me get this straight. This cat adores you and you adored it, until you found out it used to belong to your childhood bully?" Phil scoffed, obviously not finding that a good enough reason for someone to deny themself the love of a cat. He'd been wearing a dragon T-shirt at the last meeting and had a similar one with something about *Lord of the Rings* on this time. Phil clicked his tongue. "That's a real *tabby or not tabby* situation you've got on your hands, my friend."

The group groaned at the terrible pun.

"She loves you, Owen," George said, gesturing to the cat. "And you obviously like her." She motioned to the reluctant smile tugging at the corners of his mouth.

Owen set his book down and let his head flop forward in a sign of defeat. "I know," he said with an exhale. "I think I might've made a rash decision before." At this, he sent an apologetic look toward Lou.

She nodded in answer to the unspoken question he seemed to be asking with his eyes.

"I still have your paperwork and the crate you dropped her off in," Lou said.

Owen relaxed and leaned down to pick up Jules. "What do you say, girl? Do you think you could give me another chance?"

The cat purred so loudly, Lou could hear her from across the bookstore.

"Now *that's* a real *tabby or not tabby* dilemma." Phil tried again.

To which everyone at the table said, "Nope."

"Still no."

"Stop trying to make that work, Phil."

They laughed and turned back to their game. Jules curled up in Owen's lap.

Phil stopped the game a little while later with a raised finger. "You know..." Everyone shook their heads, thinking he was going to try to make that pun work again, but he said, "If you think about it, Owen, you taking his cat probably would've made Credence furious. So you're actually kind of getting back at him for all the stuff he did to you over the years."

Owen gritted his teeth. "He stuffed me inside a locker that was *not* people sized, and no one could find me for five hours."

Phil put up his hands in defense. "Just saying."

The group got back to their game.

But as Lou peeled open the book she was reading, she realized Phil was wrong. She believed Credence would be happy to see Jules was being well taken care of. He'd loved her that much. She was probably the only thing he loved in his life.

She thought about the odd poetry that was life. Credence had made Owen so miserable when they were younger, but now Owen was getting real joy from something Credence had lost.

Maybe she was the only person who felt bad for Credence's

death, but that was okay.

An hour into the D and D group's time in the shop, Timothy and Tiffany came in. Unlike each time she'd seen them separately —when they were without the babies—they came with three car seats today. Tiffany held one, and Timothy had the other two, one on each arm. Lou greeted them quieter than normal, just in case the girls were asleep.

"You brought them," she whispered excitedly as she came out from behind her checkout counter to say hello.

Timothy beamed. "No need to whisper. They're all wide awake." He snorted out a laugh.

"Which is why we brought them all in," Tiffany explained, setting her car seat down on the table.

Lou cooed to the babies as she greeted each one. Chloe, Grace, and Lola were their names, and they were each adorable.

After about a minute of fawning over the babies, the Davis parents admitted they were also in the shop because they were on a mission to find another book that the girls might learn to love just as much as *Goodnight Moon*, reporting that the two of them were quickly growing tired of that book and needed another option.

Lou offered to watch over the girls while they browsed. Little did she know how much help she would get in that endeavor. The cats sidled up to the car seats, sniffing the babies, tipping their heads adorably as they studied the little, pudgy, wide-eyed creatures.

Tiffany and Timothy left a little while later with three copies of *Llama Llama Red Pajama*, crossing their fingers that it might become a new favorite in their house.

The D and D group left soon after that. Owen stayed to get Jules all set up to come home with him again. "For good," he assured Lou.

Willow showed up just as he was leaving with Jules in tow, and she gave him an extra-hard stare to let him know he better take care of the cat. Owen seemed to understand because he nodded and scurried away from Willow.

"Almost ready?" Willow asked, walking over to where Sapphire was asleep on a stack of books. She tapped on the table until he opened his jewel-toned blue eyes and she could lean down to kiss him on the head without startling him.

Lou nodded, motioning toward the gift bag Willow held. "I just need to pick out a book for Evelyn's gift." She twiddled her fingers as she searched the shelves for the book she'd been thinking about all day for her librarian friend.

Locating the book, Lou plucked it off the shelf and took it over to the gift bag she had waiting on the counter. *The Midnight Library* by Matt Haig.

Willow frowned at the title as Lou let her read it. "Didn't you say that book was really dark?"

Lou nestled it into the bag and tipped her head to one side as she added tissue paper. "A little. But it's also quiet and intriguing. It's about a woman who's at a crossroads, kind of like our Evelyn." Lou didn't mention that the character's crossroads in the book had a lot more to do with death than retirement. She knew Evelyn would see the beauty in the story. "It makes you look at your life, your choices, and learn to let go of regrets. I think she'll love it." She clutched the bag and then looked around the shop. "Okay, now I'm ready."

Willow took the bag so Lou could lock up. But just as they started for the high school, Easton passed them on the sidewalk.

"Where are you two off to?" he asked, but Lou saw him eyeing her to make sure she was still okay after everything she'd been through on Friday.

"Evelyn Walters' retirement party," Willow said.

Easton's eyes grew wide. "She's still the librarian? Man, I thought she'd retired years ago." He shook his head.

Willow rolled her eyes, but Lou noticed there was a hint of a smile as she looked at Easton. "She's having surgery on her knee in two weeks, so she'll be out for the rest of the year on medical leave. That's why we're having her party now."

Lou was proud of Evelyn for making the decision, knowing it was the right move to put her health first.

As they stood on the corner of Thread Lane and Thimble Drive, an old junky Mustang chugged past. The convertible top was down, and Liza's blonde hair blew in the wind as she waved to Easton and the women. The car looked awful, backfiring as it went past. But from the wide grin on Liza's face, one would think she was driving the most luxurious car in the world.

"Wait. She got the car back?" Lou turned to Easton, seeing he didn't look one bit stunned.

He nodded. "They'd still been waiting on the new title information when Credence died. It wasn't in Credence's name, and wasn't part of his estate when he died. We had to revert rights back to the title holder." Easton shrugged, a smile pulling at the corners of his lips.

"That's great," Willow said. "Is she going to get it fixed up?" she added, cringing a little at how junky the thing had looked.

Easton chuckled. "I think so. She told me she wants to restore it to how it looked when her dad had it in peak condition."

Lou liked that, sure Liza's dad was proud already.

"Okay, we've gotta get going, or we're going to be late." Willow handed Lou her gift and gestured toward the high school.

Easton waved and said, "Tell Mrs. Walters congratulations for me."

The women said they would. The sun shone on them as they walked up the street. It was the kind of day that made a person want to stop, tilt their head back, and let the sunshine warm their face. So Lou did.

Until Willow pulled her along. "Come on. We're going to be late for the party."

Lou smiled and followed her friend up the street, gift bags swinging from their arms.

WHISKERS AND WORDS WILL RETURN ...

Pick up the third book in the series.

Everyone in town is *buttoned up* about the truth behind the mysterious mansion on Thread Lane.

Louisa Henry can't seem to get any answers about the abandoned mansion hidden behind brush that she runs by each day. Well, she thought it was abandoned, but she's recently seen signs of life. Whenever she asks the locals about who lives there, they clam up.

During a run, Lou notices the front door to the mysterious house is open. The body of a man lies just inside, unconscious. As Lou arrives on the scene, someone else is leaving in a hurry. Lou stays with the man only to find he's already dead, and realizes she might've just let his murderer run free.

As Lou investigates what happened, she uncovers the reason behind the man's secluded status, as well as a heap of suspects who would've wanted him dead. Can she parse the truth from the decades of lies?

Buy now!

Join Eryn Scott's mailing list to learn about new releases and sales!

ALSO BY ERYN SCOTT

A MURDER AT THE MORRISEY MYSTERY SERIES

Ongoing series * Friendly ghosts * Quirky downtown Seattle building

Pebble Cove Teahouse Mysteries

Completed series * Friendly ghosts * Oregon Coast * Cat mayors

PEPPER BROOKS COZY MYSTERY SERIES

Completed series * Literary mysteries * Sweet romance * Cute dog

STONEYBROOK MYSTERIES

Ongoing series * Farmers market * Recipes * Crime solving twins * Cats!

Whiskers and Words Mysteries

Ongoing series * Best friends *
Bookshop full of cats

About the Author

Eryn Scott lives in the Pacific Northwest with her husband and their quirky animals. She loves classic literature, musicals, knitting, and hiking. She writes cozy mysteries and women's fiction.

Join her mailing list to learn about new releases and sales!

www.erynscott.com

Made in the USA
Las Vegas, NV
26 August 2024

94432868R00125